CONUNDRUMS AND OTHER PERSONAL ESSAYS

M–Soga Mlandu

Mwanaka Media and Publishing Pvt Ltd,
Chitungwiza Zimbabwe
*
Creativity, Wisdom and Beauty

Publisher: *Mmap*
Mwanaka Media and Publishing Pvt Ltd
24 Svosve Road, Zengeza 1
Chitungwiza Zimbabwe
mwanaka@yahoo.com
mwanaka13@gmail.com
www.africanbookscollective.com/publishers/mwanaka-media-and-publishing
https://facebook.com/MwanakaMediaAndPublishing/

Distributed in and outside N. America by African Books Collective
orders@africanbookscollective.com
www.africanbookscollective.com

ISBN: 978-1-77928-532-4
EAN: 9781779285324

DISCLAIMER
All views expressed in this publication are those of the author and do
not necessarily reflect the views of *Mmap*.

Content

(i) Dedications

Special gratitude is extended to the two esteemed literary journals, Kotaz based in Gqeberha and Jack Journal from Cape Town. These journals previously published several of the essays included in this collection, providing a vital platform for the voices and stories represented herein.

(ii) Acknowledgements

Rhodes University's Institute for the Study of English in Africa (ISEA) invited me in 2013 as the Mellon Writer-in-Residence, giving me ample opportunity to refine many of these essays and to discuss my work with students, lecturers, and community members, which was a truly pleasant experience.

I am grateful to Professor Vuyisile Msila of the University of South Africa, who always provided encouraging and professional suggestions when I submitted batches of these essays for his comments.

I also thank Mr. Sithembele Isaac Xhegwana, the writer and research curator at Amazwi South African National Literature Museum, who willingly and unreservedly accepted my appeal to introduce *Conundrums and Other Essays*.

My thanks go to Advocate Mzwandile Maxwell Maraqana, who contributed credible information during my research for the essay *Honey*.

Finally, I appreciate Mr. Lusapho Mlandu, who typed and arranged the manuscript of this book.

(iii) Author's Biography

M–Soga Mlandu (1950–) was born in Mhlotsheni Village, in the district of Mount Frere, and currently resides in the suburb of North Crest in Mthatha, Eastern Cape. He is a former member of the Mayoral Committee for King Sabatha Dalindyebo Municipality, where he served as chairperson of the portfolio for Public Safety and Transport. He has published isiXhosa school books through Via Afrika, JL Van Schaik, Lovedale Press, and Vivlia, as well as English books: a collection of essays, *The Scheme and Other Essays* (Imbizo Arts Publishing, 2004); a collection of short stories, *The Tell Me Again Stories* (Lovedale Press, 2013); a collection of poems, *The Easy Patterns* (Imbizo Arts Publishing, 2015); the autobiographical novel *Things Happen for a Purpose* (His Righteousness, 2018); and another collection of essays, *A Brave Woman and Other Essays* (Austin Macauley, UK, 2024). Soga also edited *South Africa is Part of Africa* (Educall, 2000), a book of fact written by Kenyan author Dr Anthony Kambi Masha.

He translated the popular isiXhosa folksong UNogayoyo and published the text in *Botsotso Magazine* in 1999. He facilitated writers' workshops organized by the African Writers Association (AWA), Simanywa Lusiba Writers Club (Mthatha), which he co-founded and where he served as the original chairperson, Imbizo Arts Publishing, Ukhozi Press, and the Eastern Cape Department of Sports, Arts and Culture. Soga has reviewed books by Sithembele Isaac Xhegwana, Letlapa Mphahlele, and Botsotso Publishing for *Africa Books Review* and *Kotaz*.

His English and isiXhosa poems, essays, and short stories have appeared in South African commercial magazines and literary journals including *Tribute, Imprint, Botsotso, Kotaz, Timbila, Echoes , New Coin, Jack Journal*, and publications of the University of Transkei (now Walter Sisulu University) such as *UNITRA News* and *Festaac Magazine*. He has presented papers at events including the SALA Awards held in Pretoria in 2024 by DSRAC, and at the commemoration of the Eastern Cape legendary poet Mzi Mahola, held in Gqeberha in 2025 by the Nelson Mandela Bay Theatre Complex. Currently a member of the Eastern Cape Literary Society, Soga was invited in 2013 by Rhodes University's Institute for the Study of English in Africa (ISEA) as Mellon writer-in-residence and is the recipient of four South African writers awards.

(iv) Introduction

Quoting from a paper I delivered in an international conference at the Sol Plaatjie University late last year, I would like to open this introduction by raising the following points:

> I cannot help but think of a particular event in the history of my people, the amaXhosa of the Eastern Cape, when a fifteen-year old girl in particular led the whole nation into its knees. There is no other but the well-known 'prophetess' Nongqawuse, who in 1856 through the aid of her herbalist and seer uncle Mhlakaza convinced amaXhosa King Sarhili that it would be for the benefit of the amaXhosa nation to slaughter all their cattle and burn all their soil produce. This was a nail in the coffin of a nation that, between 1779 and 1879, in no particular order, had been drained by nine frontier wars; it sent the whole nation straight to the docks of Cape Town and the mines of both Johannesburg and Kimberley – a slavery of some sort.

This conundrum, for it is still a complete mystery how the whole Xhosa nation including its king fell for this well manouvered trap; this would be the beginning of both labour and brain drain through colonial subjugation to the metropoles of the time; Kimberley, Johannesburg and Cape Town. Even to the present day, voluntary or not, there is a huge exodus of amaXhosa people in particular to these urban areas. With Johannesburg as an entry point, South African 'native' literature in English has for a long time been a tourist literature (leaning mostly towards the Zulu culture which of course is in close proximity to Johannesburg). It was very rare to find isiXhosa literature or English literature written by Xhosa intellectuals until luminaries like Mzamane; Sepamla and countless others left their indelible mark in South African literature. The South African Literary Award (SALA) inaugural poet laureate, Mazisi Kunene, had long been grazing above the stars. Epics like Emperor Shaka The Great did not only plant his work as a tower in African letters but projected him to the international stage. One of course cannot forget to name great poets like the reigning SALA laureate poet, Serote, and Mphahlele who over many decades poked the National Party conceived sperate development policy.

Professor Opland's "incidental" discovery of mam'u Nontsizi Mgqwetho oeuvre within the pages of the archived *Umteteli wa Bantu*. This is also a conundrum on its own. How possible was it, at the dawn of the twentieth century, for a woman to transcend the border of "Xhosaland" to the city of gold? Is it possible that this might be a pseudonym for someone who for some reasons feared to be known? All doubt put aside, Chizama's work resonates with such elegance that it marched out of the archives to one of Professor Opland's volumes. *The Nation's Bounty* is a golden grove not only for amaXhosa but for the African child.

Let me at once say what I wanted to say. Soga Mlandu is a rare talent in South African letters. Having expressed himself through almost all genres and also being bilingual (swiftly moving between isiXhosa and English), he has been writing from the perspective of the African child whose constituency and sanctuary is the rural populace. So is the subject and theme of *Conundrums And Other Essays*, the volume I have edited. We do need to challenge the ethnographic nature of African letters where the white gazer is the appropriator of African culture and the black subject being the pathological informant. Quoting the widely circulated African idiom, "until the lion learns how to write every story will glorify the hunter". In simple terms this means that we must tell and own our stories, and not the other way around.

Sithembele Isaac Xhegwana

Amazwi South African National Literature Museum
2025

1. Conundrums

When my friend Jonga and I start our debate that is based on how the deaths of initiates that are happening at the compound on the mountainside can be prevented, things are already bad in our province in this regard. Eleven initiate deaths have been captured for this particular year alone. Also, eight initiates have already been admitted in different medical hospitals because of serious sicknesses that are related to their circumcision. Due to all this, four boys lost their manhood after their incurably damaged penises were cut off in hospital and six traditional surgeons are reported to have been arrested and then jailed for operating unlicensed initiation schools.

Adding to these hazards is a serious demand by some women in our tribal villages, townships and suburbs. The women demand to play a role at the compound on the mountainside which is actually their response to the continuous occurrence of deaths of the initiates up there before the mothers are told of their sons' bad health condition.

My argument is that all stages of the operation of this custom must involve a medical doctor who will ensure that the standards of health are not compromised during circumcision and initiation: while Jonga argues against this position with strong points.

I am basing my argument on the following facts: one, that most of the deaths of the initiates result from health related matters; two, that the present day traditional surgeons and traditional nurses that perform the custom of initiation do not do this out of their love for it but for personal gain; three, that the indigenous knowledge that was possessed by and guiding the past-time performers of the initiation has but been lost to the current performers; and four, that there is now the existence of HIV/AIDS.

The bases of Jonga's argument are as follows: one, his fear that the ethics of the custom of initiation will be put at risk for being dishonoured if services of a medical doctor are introduced at the initiation school; two, his other fear is that traditional surgeons and traditional nurses will see their function in operating the initiation custom being undermined by the nation if services of the medical doctor are introduced at the initiation school, and get frustrated and discouraged in their performance; three, he believes that the only thing that needs to be done on the mountainside is to make concrete improvements in the current ways and means of operating the initiation custom; and four, that the initiation of boys should be guided by custom: which is surely not catered for in the ways and activities of the medical doctor, who as a scientist respects dictates of his profession which are obviously opposed to the operating custom.

We have reminded ourselves about the value of the initiation custom to the initiates and to the Xhosa nation at large; and also identified the areas of its relevance to those affected. The fact that its operation assists matters of health can never be overlooked. Circumcised men are confirmed by

health institutions to have more chances to elude sexually transmitted diseases compared to the uncircumcised one. At a traditional level, the custom ens
ures that there is a specific time at which the nation dedicates its time to dictate on how a boy should handle the tribe's customs and traditions, as well as the secrets of manhood. Also, roles and responsibilities of a man to himself, his family and his nation are introduced. Consequently, this prepares the boy for the hardships that await any man in the future life. That his exposure to nature while he is kept up there opens a page for him to learn and have more knowledge of and love and respect for nature. Finally, that this custom is still popular to the current generation of boys; and that it still plays a pivotal role in uniting the amaXhosa nation, and of uniting those in the rural areas and those in the cities.

Deliberating within me before the date of the start of our debate, I say: "This problem, this, does not equal a total loss to our nation. I mean loss in dignity of our custom, in dignity of the responsible institutions and in pleasure of the parents and associates of the boy that is going to ascend the mountainside. How ugly and painful it is to know for sure that in each initiation season (June and December) the nation loses a member of its young blood? And, oh, to think of that boy who has lost the frame of his pride and his dignity – manhood! That which was the basis of his thoughts when he fantasized about himself as a future husband of a woman, a future father of a child and future head of a stead."

Explaining my position to Jonga, I first quote the words of the district surgeon of Mthatha that I previously discussed this matter with. "Although they also die because of other factors like neglect or assault by some caregivers, the initiates die there mostly because of what the care-givers call 'control of use of water' whose effects they believe quickens healing of the penis wound".

"Indeed, my friend Jonga, the interest of the current operators of this custom is based only on getting the button with no hole (money) and rivers of wine and corn beer that always flow into the *ibhoma* from the homes of the initiates and also those that are waiting for them at the homes of the initiates on the days of the celebration. Hence it is easy for the traditional nurses to even recruit the under aged boys for circumcision.

The ancient operators of the *ukwaluka* (initiation) acted like this: They first registered at the community meeting which was held at the chief's place. This is where the fitness of their knowledge about traditional affairs and values of Ubuntu (African humanity and kindness) such as respect for the seniors and protection of the young and the weak – the latter including foreigners; to participate at the initiation school was confirmed by the public. And indeed only the really credible caregivers went through this stiff sieve. Second, circumcision had no monetary value as it was actually a voluntary service. The operators saw it only as their expression of love for the community. Also, activities at the compound took place under the keenest eye of the knowledgeable men from the families of the initiates who paid regular visits up there.

And because of their resourcefulness in indigenous knowledge, the operators of the custom in the past days used healing herbs that are but no longer known by the operators of today. Let alone the huge amount of respect that the operators of those days had for their services on the mountainside.

And, indeed, there is now HIV/AIDS which uses any available opportunity to spread and to sprout. While those who live with it have a particular way of handling it the situation which urgently necessitates services of a medical doctor at the school." I tell my attentively listening friend
.

"Remember, Soga my friend. Here we are talking about a custom, which like other customs in the world has ethics that should not be offended and its dignity that should not be lowered. Hence I shuddered when in your argument you suggest participation of a medical doctor at the compound on the mountainside; the medical doctor that we have no tools to verify his cultural allegiance. Which may be hostile towards the African systems and institutions, and offend our custom of initiation," says Jonga Mjelo starting explanation of his point of argument.

"There is also something else so important that you seem to have forgotten my friend. You seem to have forgotten how pleased and honourable the caregivers show to be at the graduation ceremony at the home of an initiate when they are praised for the good service that they performed at the *bhoma* on the mountainside whose results show in success of the initiation of the son of that home. Do you think this maddening praise and resultant jubilance can be there if the caregivers' service on the mountainside was coupled by that of the medical doctor? The answer is, no. Improvement in the ways and facilities of operating this custom of ours can alone eliminate the bad situation that currently prevails at the initiation school on the mountainside. Especially by stepping up monitoring of the services of the caregivers at the initiation school by a team of culturally credible men of the family of the initiate."

After we have attended questions of clarity from both sides and laid emphasis on the urgent need for a change in the way that the custom of initiation is currently operated, my friend Jonga looks at me admiringly and says: "Your honest contribution and mine too, have made me believe that this scourge of deaths and injuries of the initiates on the mountainside can be stamped out or at least be minimized."

2. Staffrider

My brother-in-law's voice is drowning in grief, and our telephonic conversation is most unpleasant.
"Your nephew—the one who likes to visit you on school holidays, the one who recites poems to you when you are here—he risks his one and only life."
"Why do you say that?"
"He risks his one and only life."
"How does he do that?"
"He participates in a deadly exercise called train surfing, which is known as staffriding."

I am still catching my breath, easing the tension, preparing to request clarity on some parts of his subject when he suddenly cuts off the conversation, perhaps overwhelmed by strain. I quickly call him back on his cell phone so that we can continue talking.

"But who would have thought that a clever and responsible boy like Luvo could one day risk his one and only life like this?" Khulile Lukho says as our conversation continues.
I know much about this issue because I have read many stories about it in South African newspapers and magazines. Stories of tragic deaths and terrible injuries involving boys in the black townships of Johannesburg who participate in the game of jumping from one carriage to

another, spinning on poles, or even jumping onto the roof while the train is moving. These boys risk missing their target and falling, touching electric wires and getting electrocuted, colliding with walls when the train passes under bridges, or being smashed on the rails. There are also jail terms given to youths caught in the act, as well as harsh punishments meted out by train guards who, after catching them in the offense, sometimes choose not to take them to the police station.

"My wife, Nomhle, and I no longer go to bed without taking stress pills. The boy has brought a long-bladed spear into our house," Khulile concludes, terribly downhearted.

His younger sister, my wife Tutula, is loading airtime onto her cell phone to contact the boy's parents when I phone my brother-in-law to inform him about our decision to visit them the next Saturday. The taxi transporting us to Johannesburg behaves as if it understands the urgency of our visit—it speeds through 900 kilometre distance and gets us to our destination right on time.

I look at him as he meets us at the gate, relieving us of some of our bags. Luvo is still the same boy I have known since the time he wore a bib and drank milk from a bottle, up to his current age of 15. He quickly smiles on his ebony face and still uses both hands when greeting a visitor. A typical African child!

"I love the game, my uncle. It challenges my energy, promotes nimbleness of my limbs, stimulates my brain, and through it I fulfil my sports desires," he says meekly. The small sitting room feels as if it has acoustics because of the quietness between speeches. I clear my throat and ask,

"Have you considered the deadly risks involved in this game?"

"That is exactly where I started, my uncle. Actually, I first studied the game thoroughly by observing the participants tirelessly. I noted their shortcomings and analysed the successes of those who managed it safely for a long time. I also interviewed former participants who retired before facing major hazards." Luvo displays confidence in himself, commitment to the game, and respect for us.

I announce a short break so we can cool off before diving deeper into the matter. Droplets of sweat have already appeared on my brother-in-law's face even before the meeting I chair starts. He constantly grinds his teeth silently. Apparently the break feels too long for my brother-in-law because as soon as we are back, even before I invite contributions, he raises his hand to speak. He shows us recent statistics on the hazards of train surfing from a newspaper he has carried under his armpit. He also presents programmes from funeral services of victims of this game which he attended. The newspapers reveal instances of Luvo's involvement in trouble while participating in train surfing.

Continuing, my brother-in-law says, "Two things worry me most about Luvo's involvement in this risky game: first, his portrayal of it as a good thing, which I fear will keep his ears sealed to our advice; and second, the thought that if he continues, it may one day influence his younger brother Sandi to join him. That would only complicate this problem we're trying to solve."

After his father's talk, Luvo tries once more to humble us but instead invites more questions from me:

"When it became known at home—through an instance of my bad luck—that I had been in this game a long time without accident, I established where I went wrong and have already eliminated the weakness that caused my failure."

"Have you also identified where you might go wrong next time?" I ask softly.

"I think that was the only weakness, uncle. That was the last stunt we performed," he answers confidently.

"Do you know all the dangers in this game that can injure or kill a participant?" I keep my eyes fixed on him.

"I don't think there are any more pitfalls to emerge in this game, my dear uncle," he replies with a serious expression.

"But what makes you sure there are no dangers you have yet to face?" I probe patiently. He does not answer but merely scuffs the floor with the tip of his right shoe.

Looking at him with both forceful and beseeching eyes, Tutula shifts her medium-sized body and says, "I, your father's sister, your aunt, belong to those in society who use few words expecting a straight, brief answer. So, can you tell us, what trouble will you experience if you immediately stop participating in this kind of adventure?" Luvo looks down and then up, answering, "Err… Err… I don't know what to say beyond what I said earlier, my aunt." Tutula asks no more questions. She folds her arms and shifts her eyes from Luvo uneasily.

We listen attentively as Luvo's younger brother, Sandi, tells how Luvo got involved in staffriding: "…Among his classmates is a boy lovingly called Big Boss for championing staffriding. Luvo is the only one among Grade Eleven learners who beats Big Boss academically. Not satisfied with being second in the class, and actually despising ever being beaten in studies (which had never happened before), Big Boss worked harder to reclaim the top spot. He increased his study time, frequented school and municipal libraries, and consulted teachers for clarity and guidance on difficult subjects. Big Boss pursued his goal resolutely until Luvo declared, 'I will beat him in everything!' Luvo then decided to join staffriding.

After some months, when every learner knew that Luvo had performed all the stunts of staffriding in one trip to town, and faster than Big Boss or any other performer, the former champion refused to meet anyone's gaze in dismay. Meanwhile, Luvo was congratulated by everyone at school," Sandi concludes.

Before our meeting closes, Luvo's mother Nomhle shifts her bulky yet light body in her armchair and asks him, "Do you know how a mother feels when her child is involved in a dangerous exercise like staffriding?"
His eyes twinkling with seriousness, Luvo replies, "I really don't know, my beloved mother."
"A mother feels as if she herself is in that danger; she even foresees the pains her child will suffer when a mishap occurs. These pains torment her soul and emotions just as they do the body and soul of the child. This stops only if the child withdraws immediately from that terrible exercise," his mother concludes. Luvo says nothing, only lifts his eyes and looks above our heads, pitifully.

"We really have to stop Luvo from risking his delicate body against the moving train and the hard surfaces of the earth!" I say to Tutula as we whisper about the meeting we held in Soweto the previous day, while the bus we are traveling in hums and drones, ascending hills, descending slopes, and crossing plains, taking us back to Mthatha.

Shortly after our return from Soweto, we hear from my brother-in-law that Luvo intends to visit us during the December holidays, which are fast approaching. "…This time he had no plans to visit you, but we persuaded him so that we can have a moment of relief from the stress and strain his involvement in staffriding causes us. We also hope his interaction with youths who do not participate in this dangerous activity will inspire him to develop interest in healthier hobbies," my brother-in-law explains.
"Moreover, we don't have passenger trains here, only goods trains," I add, supporting Luvo's intended visit.

On the second day after his arrival, Luvo comes to my small library where I'm filing paper cuttings and assists me willingly. After we finish, resting in the sitting room, he coughs softly and begins narrating what he calls his progress in staffriding.
"They have now made me their coach," he reveals.
"Doesn't that put you in even greater danger?" I ask before he   finishes.
"But, my uncle, I cannot do that without physically participating in the game," he answers. His reply diminishes my interest in the conversation, and I respond only with nasal agreements until he changes the topic.

That evening, after my son Dike and Luvo return from the bus stop where they fetched Sandi, Luvo's younger brother, who is traveling to Cape Town but staying overnight with us before continuing, the boys have a loud, jubilant conversation in Dike's room. Their rooms are close, and windows half-closed due to summer heat, allowing me to overhear as I leisurely thumb through an isiXhosa book I bought months ago at a Port Elizabeth book fair.

"...There is virtually no difference between staffriding and mountain climbing, which is lavishly funded by relevant institutions, or between staffriding and the Spanish sport of bull chasing, in terms of risk. And don't talk about those who ride waves on ski boards in violent seas! My booking for an appointment with officials in the national Department of Recreation, Sports, Arts, and Culture to discuss recognition of staffriding has been successful," Luvo says between breaths, beating his broad chest amid cheers.
Offended by what Luvo said and by the enthusiastic response of others, an unexplainable storm rises inside me, straining my soul. Tutula comes into the sitting room and shares my disturbance. After stopping her from confronting the boys about their discussion, I begin narrating the origin of staffriding.

"It started in the 1950s with tsotsis from Johannesburg's black townships, soon joined by schoolboys who couldn't afford train tickets for trips to and from town due to poverty or because they mischievously spent money given by their parents or guardians. It later became a popular illegal sport practiced mainly by schoolboys who adopted it as a hobby, despite knowing the risks involved." Tutula nods appreciatively, suppressing intermittent sobs from recent anger.

Two weeks have passed since Luvo's return. My wife and I prepare to visit his home to report to his parents on our observations of his behaviour so we can plan the next step to solve this problem. Then my brother-in-law's phone call wakes us from sleep.

His long stammering and extreme coarseness tell me something bad has happened. "My son... Your nephew... My son and the train. Oh, my son!" I immediately try to comfort Tutula, who listens attentively as my cellphone speaker transmits the conversation, before she bursts into hysterical crying, joined by our son.

I pity the boy's parents for their loss, our loss. Pity them for the loss they foresaw and struggled so hard to prevent but could not. And I weep for the loss of Luvo—the top quality boy, with his gifts and attributes.

3. The Hornets' Nest

Even now, I have to follow my father's she-goat almost all day throughout the autumn. This is what I must do every year, as this brown and black-headed she-goat has a habit of hiding her kid after giving birth and returning home from the veld alone. On the same day she gives birth, the she-goat starts giving her kid orders. Then, through a certain inconceivable animal language, she begins teaching it to obey them. One of the orders is to hide under rocks or beneath some bushy shrubs. When she is sure the kid understands and obeys the orders, she leaves it and returns home for the night.

As they are alone in the veld, many things transpire between the two animals. The she-goat leads her kid to suck from her udder, which almost kisses the ground—nudging it tenderly with her face, but also kicking it impatiently if it continues to suck at her teats after she has told it to stop. The kid twists its short tail rhythmically from side to side while it joyfully sucks its mother's milk. It sometimes also teases her by poking her with its hornless head. Then the two animals lie side by side on their bellies, sharing warmth through their bristles.

She sometimes leaves her kid in the wild for a few days or weeks because she does not trust humans for the kid's safety. She also hates dogs for their barking and the look of plunder in their eyes. She chooses to let her kid grow up in the wild until it can move properly and look after itself. When she arrives back home with it—sometimes still moving unsteadily on its soft hooves behind her and dropping milky dung—she stamps the ground with her foreleg hoof. If she sees dogs approaching her walking treasure, she angrily attacks them with her two upward-pointing horns. Before she scratches the ground with her hoof to prepare to lie down for the night (as goats like to do), she first looks around for their enemies.

The she-goat has now returned from the veld with reduced weight, showing traces of blood on her hindquarters. She is tired and restless. After dropping a few pellets of dung and scratching the surface of the earth, she lies down, resting her tired body. "This goat has again given birth in the wild and left it there," I murmur and sigh. The inherent and understandable joy that the goat has increased my father's wealth is mixed with irritation and anger. I have already started imagining what a challenging task it will be to follow her in the veld day after day to discover where her kid is hidden so I can retrieve it for my father.

The newly born kid is now part of my father's wealth. It has to be brought home. Also, I am anxious for the kid's safety since the bushes near Mhlotsheni Village harbour jackals, African wild cats, and iingqawa. The following morning, I open my father's kraal gate and drive the goats out for the day's grazing. I keep an eye on the brown and black-headed she-goat because I have a plan to save myself much trouble.

Immediately after leaving the kraal, she breaks away from the flock, following a separate path. Her ears drooping and eyes cast to the ground, she searches for her little path. The flock moves toward the gently sloping eastern part of the nearby bush, while she walks steadily south toward the hills, apparently lost in her thoughts. It is a bright, clear day without a cloud in the sky and just a faint breeze—perfect weather to track a goat, I silently think to myself.

I let her walk for a while, then break away from the herd myself and, without her noticing, circle around toward a huge old tree on the outskirts of the bush. Hidden from her, I climb into its thick boughs to monitor her movements and moods. Almost as soon as I get sight of her, I have to clamber quickly down because she has started trotting in yet another direction, this time toward a thicket of thorn trees. By the time I have climbed down, she has disappeared. Blocked by brambles and scratched by thorns, I force my way into the thorn thicket where I saw her slip in—my eyes on the ground to track her hoofprints and my ears alert to the sound of her movements or the bleat of her kid.

In a clearing, she suddenly slows and starts browsing on the soft, low-hanging tree leaves and succulents, as if she does not harbour a care in the world. I suspect she wants to check if I am following her. I keep very still and watch. I believe her destination is nearby and brace myself for the excitement of discovering the kid's hiding place. When she moves on again, I drop and crawl as quietly as I can. Suddenly, she turns and runs fast past me, brushing aggressively against the branches of the short trees to my left. As if by magic, a swarm of angry hornets fills the air. Later, I realise that she has intentionally stirred their nest. I turn and, bending low, run for my life, my arms held up to protect my eyes from thorns. Even in the thicket, they repeatedly sting my face and head.

When I eventually outrun the thicket and the swarm, I sit down and tenderly rub my palms over the painful areas of my face and head to soothe them. I think of my responsibility to the flock. The worst of the pain subsides, and eventually, I am able to go in search of her again. I find her travelling through an area of the bush where the fleshy-leafed trees are tall and touching their neighbours, so sometimes you can't tell which branch belongs to which tree. The forest still retains the coolness of the previous night. Tree leaves cup the dew drops left by the morning mist. Hence a soft gum trickles down over the bark of some trees, and I can smell a beautiful mix of perfumes from various kinds of flowers. These attract some long-beaked and long-tailed birds, as well as large butterflies from the koppies.

The she-goat is enjoying the new, steeper terrain that opens up as we climb into the sunshine. It becomes rocky with huge boulders and brilliant orange and red aloes growing between the crevices. She moves with agility and speed, demonstrating this is her natural habitat, not mine. She seems to be playing a game of jumping from one stone to the next in ever-increasing leaps, easily widening the distance between us.

I am losing touch with her, so I revert to my previous tactic and climb a tree. Still jumping from rock to rock for a few minutes, she seems to be enjoying her own acrobatics.

Then she unexpectedly turns down toward the banks of the Umzimvubu River that is gurgling peacefully below as it flows past our village. I sit there in the boughs and watch her bend her forelegs and sip to quench her thirst. I then realise how thirsty I am.

From there, she takes another circular route back to the bush area where the rest of my father's flock is grazing. But to me, she looks discontent. She is tense; the bristles raise from her ever turned-up tail to her head. Her appearance reminds me of any mother who has been away from her baby, now panicking for its safety. She lets out a bleat, just once—mistakenly or on purpose—I can't tell. She constantly sneezes wildly, her long and pointed ears erect.

I reluctantly climb down the tree. As I approach my father's herd, I see traces of her leaking milk on the ground and on the flat stones. When I am close enough to her, I see her full udder hanging painfully between her hindquarters. "Let me show her that I have discarded my plan to follow her," I think, and sprint past her to the rest of the flock. I have been defeated by the clever old she-goat, but that is not what concerns me. I feel very bad for delaying the necessary meeting of the two animals. When she is sure I have learnt my lesson, she turns back toward the thorn thicket, and I let her go alone.

4. Left School Earlier

When I pass by people suffering from the pangs of lesser or no formal education, especially road workers when they are digging into hard ground with picks in the heat of a summer's day or being whipped by icy winter winds, I usually halt and think deeply, tortured inside by the thought that I nearly became one of them. Let alone that these people may see nothing wrong with their lot. Indeed, having left before even obtaining a Standard Six Certificate, I am sure to be doomed to work in mines or clean city streets – not to lift the pen and express ideas. However, like many of these struggling masses, one must take note that there are a number of things that made me bid school goodbye with no certificate in hand.

Besides measuring fifteen kilometres, the land through which my way cuts from home in Mhlotsheni village to the higher primary school in Lutateni village (both villages being in Mount Frere District) is laced with rocky hills, spreading out plains with pastures and mealie-fields, strips of built-up areas, and curling brooks. By all means, that is the way waiting for my feet to pound throughout all schooling days of the year.

The effects of path-pounding are not felt only by my limbs, but also by the pair of tennis shoes that I wear. Every third month, my parents have to purchase a new pair of tennis shoes for me, their schooling boy, their last born. And, oh, how proud I am to be one of only nine boys in the overcrowded big school who wear a pair of shoes!

What about available means of traveling? Oh yes, my father owns a herd of horses and a mule, but I rarely travel on any of those. To get them next to the bridle and the saddle is a tiresome activity. They graze far away from home and are wild. Nor will I travel on the bicycle as my father discourages his four sons, including myself, from even thinking about that, claiming traveling on that skeletal thing is not dignified.

Also, vehicles are almost non-existent in this area in these days, at least for me. The one bus that is there is always traveling in the direction opposite to mine; and it is uncommon to think of taxis here in the Sixties in the tribal villages. We only see the smoky and noisy cars that occasionally come in, hired by people who work in the cities or owned by the boyfriends of our working aunts. That is all about the machine called taxi.

Staying next to the school, too, is impossible for me. My schooling does not relieve me of my daily chores at home. Every afternoon or evening on my arrival, and every morning before I leave, I have to go to the kraals and check if there is no beast missing, and this pleases my father extensively. Seeing that I am as responsible and as observant as the African proverb that says a man is a man because he possesses livestock. Of course, that is his livestock. My love for my parents and my home environment can't allow me to sleep far away, even for a day. But the tiredness. Oh, the tiredness! It befriends my body and my brain!

The weather conditions, with unpredictability and heavy arm, are an ever-present pester. Bad weather evades and overcomes all the protection I have and troubles me so much. Indeed, even though my parents arm me with all kinds of protective clothing and the school takes its responsibility by releasing me at the emergence of dark clouds and condoning my absence on days of bad weather, and villagers along the way willingly offer shelter, the elements don't lack ways to reach me. The first feet to break the droplets of the dew or the crust of the frost and the sure face to be sjamboked by the afternoon winds are mine.

There is also this day, a certain Friday. The nimbus ascends from the sea and seals off the sky, the wind bends everything low, and the rain cascades upon the ground. I press myself against a crumbly wall of a riverbank, and before my confusion and convulsion subside, I find myself floating among the waves as the fast-flowing brown water twirls and twists both banks of the river. Thanks so much that I can battle and I am so light to be fortunately spitted onto the bank, at the river's bend.

"How did you cross?" an unknowing stranger asks the boy who is standing still like a statue and looking at his school bag that is bobbing about among the logs and waves southwards.

My teacher in the higher primary school is one of those who believe that a learner can achieve good marks only if he/she is nudged through a rod, and that a misbehaving pupil can be corrected only by the use of the same tool. I wish that I will always remember the words of the praise-song he sings as he whips all failures in every test, all late-comers, and all noise-makers in the Standard Five Class so that I can quote them whenever I talk about this. Even the repeaters whom I am going to join the following year always receive multiplied punishment. It is through this that I lost a friend to the coal-mines. "I don't want to cross the school ground again," he said, showing me some bluish marks on his left hand.

What made it better in the lower primary school is that the pupils of four classes (Standard 1, 2, 3, and 4) were together under one roof and taught by one teacher. That way we could dodge the rod sometimes. At lower primary school, children from one home took turns – this one today and that one the following day, regardless of which grade each was in. One had to look after the livestock while the other went to school, but all this is not here in the higher primary school, so the rod always lands on one's flesh.

In my village, most of the boys of my age are already working and can boast effectively about their financial independence from their parents. "This watch, this suit, and this pair of shoes I bought with money from my own pocket. I don't ask for money from my parents – they ask for it from me. Now I'm saving enough lobola which will assist me in a few years from now to find myself a permanent partner," one of them says, with his finger pointing to whatever he is referring to.

At the time, I do not see much value in the importance of education. I see it only as a tool to make one speak others' language, and wear like they do, not as a liberator. I have an example of this at my home. My elder sister Nombuyiselo

Eugenia Mlandu, a professional teacher who loves her job so much, but always comes home with a cheque for a too small amount compared to what my father, who left school in Standard Two (Grade Four), makes a month from selling maize from his fields and payments after building others' houses or fencing their gardens. Because of his kraals that are rocking with bleats and bellows and his barns that are bulging with crop, my father enjoys a higher status in the community compared to my sister.

In January, as school opens, I have no reason to prepare my school bag. I am preparing to go to the labour recruitment office in the nearby town of Mount Frere.

But will I succeed? Let me state that by all means I am setting my feet on virgin territory. "Today we are selecting workers for Bethal potato farms in Transvaal. We need eighty-two recruits," a smartly dressed clerk explains over a loudspeaker while standing on the office's veranda.

At hearing this, my eyebrows began lifting stealthily while scratching my head; I move backwards. I have heard many frightening stories and witnessed many pathetic cases of inhuman treatment of workers from the Bethal potato farms. Those who eventually escape arrive home with no nails on their fingers – because of digging with their hands – and scars are visible all over their bodies – punched by the prisoners who are bought by the farmers from jail (as this is allowed by the law of the time), or bitten by the hounds that are set on them when they are found trying to escape.

"At least to somewhere else," I think to myself as I turn my toes towards the bus rank to home. Some people in the village see benefit in my non-schooling. They show this by words to my parents: "Can the boy drive my beasts to the veld?" "I have come to borrow the boy to take money to my child in the junior secondary school across a few rivers."

My parents portray their disapproval of my discontinuation of schooling but in different ways. My mother Mary Jane Nondima MaRhadebe Mlandu shows an exaggerated kindness – calling me with the tender names she would use when I was still a child or buying me something new each time she goes to the shops. "My son, you are but too tiny to lift the heavy articles that are lifted on the mines, even on the harbours or on sugar plantations. We are aging and moreover our wealth is waning. The little we have we would like to spend paying for your education so that you can fend for yourself easily in adulthood," my mother explains.

Looking at me with war-fevered eyes and avoiding by all means talking to me, my father Jacob Msebenzi Mlandu suddenly roars to my mother: "This boy, we wanted to give him the wealth that no storm can destroy, and no thief can steal! And which will make him look at the world with an expanded sight. I mean the one which, when obtained, is never lost. Tell him I have no space here for this boy who has left school; he must pack and go away! Now!"

Having seen and heard all this, I feel a strange feeling inside me – a feeling of missing my schoolmates and the environment of my higher primary school, especially the face of the blackboard. Realizing this, I whisper to my mother: "Tell tata I'm returning behind the desk."

Now, even if I have the capacity, I will not try to establish what I will gain and what I will lose culturally by possessing the specialized knowledge called "education." I am in a hurry to resume my schooling.

And my bag, fully stuffed with books, feels so light in my hand.

5. Unidentified

Many factors contribute to the elusiveness of our search for the dead body of Mr Ndoda Ndingida. Insisting on the search within politically spiraled hostel war only compounds the problem.

"When on the 1st of September 1990 Ndoda Dingida was reported missing, war in men's hostels between members of two political organizations had long started, with its horrifying effects. The war had already spilled over into the townships and squatter settlements, making travelling unsafe. On the previous day, he clocked in for work and clocked out for departure back to the men's hostels," the official of the goldmine where Ndoda worked before his disappearance tells us, leaning forward across the brown table in his office. Dora, my cousin, who is the wife of the 34-year-old missing man, and I nod often as the man talks, acknowledging the information that he is sharing with us.

"Actually, the war has created a killer zone between the hostel and the workplace. On a daily basis, workers get killed or injured by the enemy while climbing down from taxis, buses, or trains. Deaths and absences of workers at work cause countless losses for the business," pressing his small-lipped mouth, the official concludes. Some of the things he is telling us we have read in newspapers and heard about on the small FM radio that we are carrying with us.

Indeed, travelling is unsafe throughout the City of Gold. We have witnessed this with our naked eyes. On the morning of this same day, some people were forced to throw themselves out of the windows of a moving train. Luggage and school bags flew about in the air before landing on the ground and being damaged or picked up by passers-by. Fierce fighting started between members of the Gagawu Party and those of the Zazawu Party. When the train stopped at the next station, our lungs were banging hard against our rib cage. Some travellers sustained injuries while others died instantly upon hitting the ground or on contact with a bullet or assegai.

I really shall not forget what we encountered at Hloko-hloko hostel where Ndoda had stayed. The memory still sends icy cold and spasms through my body. "When you arrive home, you must slaughter a white goat thanking your ancestors for your narrow escape. Death missed you by an inch. It is only an hour after the panga and gun battle stopped. Perhaps you saw the fleet of ambulances and hearses on your way here. If you like, you can come into the yard of this hostel to see for yourselves pools of fresh blood and ugly marks on the walls that were inscribed by bullets from the AK47s and R1 rifles that they used in the battle. And the journalist who was here to cover the event perished on the edge of a spear," one of the security guards looking after the empty hostel tells us on our arrival at the gate. We leave immediately, talking only with frightened eyes, forcing forward our benumbed feet.

Nights supersede days as far as the lack of safety is concerned. "We are told they are coming. Let's immediately rush to the hiding place!" one leader in the township where we are residing with relatives commands. And we don't ask who the "they" are or where the hiding place is. We only do what the others do and follow the flow to the destination which turns out to be the cemetery. We hear the cracking of guns and see sparks that travel across space from both sides. I fear babies will cry in a way that can expose us, but the opposite happens. "Perhaps mothers have their secret way of achieving this!" I whisper within my shivering self when dawn arrives and we stream back to our respective homes.

Actually, sleep refuses to come to me the whole lengthy night, not because of discomfort due to the nature of our hiding place or fear of the ensuing war. No. I am trying to figure out how this war happened. My thinking is based on the fact that there are more reasons for these people not to go to war than reasons for them to go to war against each other. They are equal victims of the ugly history of apartheid. They belong to common church denominations, many have their in-laws and cousins across the ideological line. Also, both sides are destined to be prospective beneficiaries of the freedom that is hatching in the country.

When my thinking process ends, I pronounce my belief within me. "Through what is called ideology, the people's activity named politics has enormous power with which it divides people. And sometimes, especially during the race towards elections, it fills them with hate which deprives them of individual thinking and acting. Politics! That is.

Information that we receive from an officer at a police station in one of the black townships in Johannesburg does not only horrify us. It also reveals factors that set barriers to the success of our search. "Indeed, we collected dead bodies of the victims from the scenes of death and rushed them to government mortuaries and to private mortuaries when the former were full. At some stage, when all the local mortuaries were full, some dead bodies were brought here and piled up in the backyard of the station so that we had an opportunity to arrange with mortuaries in areas outside Johannesburg to come and collect them.

At one hospital, we are told a shocking thing: some wards are occupied by victims brought in by hijacked ambulances. Explaining this, the nurse says: "We sent out ambulances to areas from which we had received calls requesting the services of these specialized cars. But on their way to specified destinations, the ambulances were stopped forcefully and diverted to places that we had no deal with and loaded with victims that we had not been told of, with the words saying 'We cannot endure to see our friends and relatives groaning or dying from pains of bullet wounds while the ambulances that could save them from pain or death pass by to other places!' Such is the character of the violent situation!"

Identification of some corpses cannot succeed. Many dead bodies are headless, some having joined with parts that did not belong with them, and some are bloated with swelling and turned pitch-black because of prolonged exposure lying in the simmering sun of the summer. The absence of persons' IDs on their lifeless bodies has complicated the problem." When he finishes his talk, we are already dumb with wonder and worry.

Our search in hospitals is notorious for raising unnecessary hopes, a factor which saps energy from our bodies and torments our souls. We first move eagerly and with wide strides from ward to ward following the nurse who is taking us to people whose speech was impaired or deadened by the severity of their head injuries while they do not have identity documents with them. Instead of joy, this exercise always strikes us with disappointment.

After many visits to our local magistrate at Centane, we decided to continue the body's search in Johannesburg. We witnessed dead bodies delivered by trucks from Johannesburg for relatives to identify. If successfully identified, they went through a tedious claiming process and were eventually buried.

"We want to see his dead body, cry over it, burry it and find consolation," Dora said as she requested me to accompany her to Johannesburg to conduct the search. We are still moving from mortuary to mortuary where we patiently page and scrutinize the discoloured, decomposed, bloated, or beheaded bodies that are piled up here when the state declares the date and place for the common burial of the unidentified bodies of the victims of the hostel war. This actually brings us relief from the pangs of tension that hold us in their grip.

The 30-year-old woman in my company has already developed new habits. She commonly talks loudly to herself, grinds her teeth as if she is chewing the wind, and forgets what she said, forgets what she did.

We have already sprinkled soil onto all the coffins, in rows, with the dead bodies of the unidentified victims in the common grave at the Avalon Cemetery in Soweto, when Mrs Dingida says: "I now know how to answer my two children when, growing up, they ask me where we buried their dear father. And I know my status; I am a widow and I am the breadwinner." Adding to her words I say, "Fare you well, unidentified relative!"

6. On Coming Back Home

We have enjoyed the return of my cousin from exile, but only for a while. Gugu Gangata himself says, "I sometimes fail to understand which act was wiser, between my coming back home and my staying in exile on unbanning in this country of all the political organizations that were previously banned, including mine."

We know his displeasure today, on his big day. And it actually spoils the welcome-home ceremony we are holding today at his home in his honour. The family and residents of Cala are already seated under the tent pitched on the yard of his home, expecting him to emerge from the newly built flat in his brand new black suit, coming to take a seat next to his widowed mother, Nontombi, my aunt, who is already seated at the table. Then Gugu does a shocking thing. We wait patiently for him to come for the start of the event's program, but nothing happens. Until we send his brother Sipho to tell him we have long been ready to start. Instead of coming back with him, Sipho asks me to rush to the flat.

I find the man of the event lying on his stomach on his bed, his arms stretched out limply, his tear-drenched face covered with the corner of the duvet, his body momentarily shaking pitifully. "Two things happened my cousin. The message is in my cellular phone. The wife is divorcing me, and the child is in hospital having attempted to commit suicide. Oh, my child! Oh, my marriage!" he says between sobs. After a long session of comforting and encouraging him, Gugu rises and goes to the tent where he is expected to narrate about his life in exile and reveal the role he intends to play in liberated South Africa. Instrumental and choral music groups take turns gracing the event. His speech grips the young and the old—who sometimes laugh, sometimes cry.

Days later, Gugu narrates to us about his funny wedding in exile. Talking about this, he says, "The people who were attending the wedding and frustrated at the station waiting for the bus that was behind its schedule were not aware that the bridegroom was in fact there among them: more frustrated than they were. I had been delayed by the person who took long to reduce the size of the jacket that I had borrowed from my friend to wear together with the trousers that I was bought for by my parents before I went into exile. I had also not been quick in dying my shoes from white to black. And it was hard for me to endure the pains at the thought of the bride who was anxiously waiting at the church in company of her parents and her friends: waiting for the groom who was still far away and stuck." We look at him in disbelief, pain, and pity.

The problem also shows up at the place of his newly found job. "We are appealing to you, sir, as his cousin: to tell him that he is loved and admired by his seniors, his equals and his subordinates here at his work because of his good character and diligence. And to make him aware that readers of our popular newspaper, too, admire him most for his good pen. He always doesn't come back in time when he visits his family in Botswana." The words of the Chief

Editor of the Abantu Weekender he is working for ring loud in my mind, and I immediately act as requested.

Having armed himself with degrees in journalism from Makerere and Botswana universities through funding from the UNO, where he also encountered African academics of note and world-acclaimed authors, Gugu is lining up well with the powerful South African journalists that write for the Abantu Weekender. I love his articles and always add them to the paper cuttings bursting from my files. I like his style and appreciate the wealth of facts he provides.

I still have a clear memory of the day I noticed his absence at Rhode High School in Mount Ayliff, where I was his senior. We were queuing patiently on the veranda of the school building to receive school books and other academic materials to begin the school calendar year when I noticed he was not there in the queue among students of his class. "He has skipped the country into exile in Lesotho," his friend whispered in my ear, shocking me madly.

I then remember what he would say when we History boys secretly discussed the scourge of racial apartness, commonly known as apartheid, which was at its boiling point at that moment. Venting his anger, he would say, "To succeed, the liberation struggle requires sacrifice, and sacrifice." He has now sacrificed his education, his youth, his togetherness with family, and sight of the physical environment of his beautiful country. Tears of anger or pity would always fill his bold eyes when he said these words. He was also a fan of the school drama group that acted Alan

Paton's political novel, Cry the Beloved Country, in which I participated.

Lerato, his wife and mother of their two children—the boy and the girl—is clear and factual in her words to Gugu about her stand on going with him and their children to South Africa.

"You did not tell me how you prepared your family in Cala to receive a daughter-in-law whose left leg vanished when the military camp of your organization, which included our residence, was attacked by your enemy during their cross-border raid with bombs and bazookas." Up to now, Gugu has still failed to respond to Lerato's question, and has not told her why.

"I avoid engaging in any discussion that may compel me to talk about your disability. As you know, talking about it—even before I start doing that—pains me inside, drowns my voice in grief, and eventually causes me to fall into fainting fits. All this is caused by my remembrance that you were injured during your time of sacrifice, staying with me in my organization's military camp where the attack of the enemy was always not an unexpected incident. And to think that you already sacrificed a lot by loving and then finally marrying an exile, myself—somebody who owns nothing, who himself entirely depends on his political organization for everything—even a piece of soap to wash his face. It kills me inside to recall that you got injured and disabled when South Africans were attacking South Africans inside Botswana, your country." Lerato listens to this with mixed feelings—feelings of pity for what Gugu said, and also feelings of urgency to get a response to her previously asked question.

On falling in love with Gugu, Lerato, the social worker and daughter of a bank manager (her father) and a professional nurse (her mother), left the warmth of her home and stayed with her sweetheart in the military camp. She didn't complain when on one occasion Gugu delayed returning from South Africa where he and two others had been commanded to perform a military assignment and then had a steel-against-steel contact with the South African army forces, which resulted in him sustaining a bullet wound above his knee that took long to heal, receiving secret medical treatment at the safe house arranged by internal operatives of his organization.

Talking about Gugu's poverty, the Bishop of the Roman Catholic Church who officiated their marriage said, "This is my second time in my calling to officiate a marriage where the bridegroom is an unspeakably poor person. The first was in Germany where the bride was the daughter of a wealthy family and the groom a young Irish soldier of the liberation struggle who owned nothing except the love for his country. What I am going to say here is what I said at that unforgettable event: that, in my knowledge, marriages of this nature are unshakeable. Nothing is able to break them."

The other thing that Gugu does answering Lerato's question is using every trick he can think of to make her change her stance and immediately come to South Africa with their children to join him. Making an appeal to her, he likes kneeling at her feet, lifting his hands up as if in prayer, and crying with his mouth, his eyes, his face, and his body. But Lerato remains unshaken.

He also exaggerates situations in his narrations aiming to lure Lerato to him in South Africa. Talking about the one room he is renting in a flat that he shares with other tenants, he says, "this flat that I am rented for by my bosses has these magnificent features: the four bedrooms—one for us, one for our kids, one for the helper, and one for visitors. Within it is a kitchen and two bathrooms with toilet facilities. There is also an evergreen lawn and bubbling swimming pool before it, as well as a balcony that provides a view of the sea and interesting bushes." Lerato listens to this during their telephonic conversation, but with too much hesitation.

Eventually, I find the Abantu Weekender I bought empty of the articles penned by Gugu. "Have they dismissed him at the press? Or has he failed to return after visiting his family in Botswana?" I ask myself, puzzled and pained. I am soon answered on a weekend, while at Jan Smuts Airport in Johannesburg. I am paging through a Botswana magazine and find its editor-in-chief to be no one else but Gugu Gangata.

On one of his many visits back home in Cala, he is not alone but in the company of members of his young family. He repeats the words he said at the gate of his home two years earlier on his arrival from exile, as we had run to the gate to meet him on his appearance there: "I feel blessed when on returning after fifteen years in exile I find my home not bare of its occupants, my relatives. I had a fearsome thought of finding it an empty site with untraceable pegs, which horrified me intensely throughout my long journey back here. It indeed pleases me greatly to find it with people to receive me on my return. I mean people to relate to about my experiences in exile; people to show the wounds I sustained and the gains I made in that wilderness. Also, your presence at this home has saved me from the unpleasant situation which is currently affecting many returnees: that of staying at a repatriation camp, which is not much different from the bad life we lived in exile, and as it also entails the risk for us former soldiers of the liberation struggle of being attacked by ill-disciplined elements in the ranks of our former foes."

He then informs us that he has decided to be a citizen of two countries: that of his birth and that of his former life as an exile. To which his mother, Nontombi, responds, advising him, "To be exact, we have always pitied you for your regular long journeys between the two countries; in your honest attempt to please both ends. I am therefore happy to inform you that your family here advises you to concentrate your efforts on the care and development of your young family."

After these words, we all stand up and engage in hearty, tearful hugs—with the constant rattle of crutches from Gugu and members of his young family. Silence fails to muffle the sobs and sighs rocking the room.

7. Day of the Cow

Mvenyane's lowing and running around the yard perplex us at home, attract the attention of neighbours and passers-by, and invite barking and chasing from dogs. The thuds of her hooves and tremors in the ground send pigs and fowls into hiding—the yard becomes temporarily bare of the small living things.

Her tail is up—its brush wavering terribly in the air behind her, her head lowered—sharp pointed horns aiming forward menacingly, ears erect and eyes protruding fiercely. Waves of fear or anger course visibly beneath her brown and white skin. I hardly blink as I study Mvenyane's strange behaviour and unbecoming appearance.

Never before has this cow returned from the grazing land just an hour after she and the other cattle from my father's two kraals were driven there.

The lowing of the cow across the sky between the two hills overlooking our village settlement on the slope persists, awakening us to something beyond our human comprehension. Mvenyane still behaves like this when I shout at her—alerting her that I have understood the message she is communicating to us at home with her strange behaviour. Problem in the veld! She then exits our unfenced yard.

Fighting sticks are held up, our heels nearly touch our backs, our chests pushed forward as my three friends and I run after her while she speeds across the plain field between our settlement and the nearby bushes to see what has befallen my father's beasts or her calf in the grazing land since she has returned home alone.

We try hard to keep close behind her but fail as she increases her speed—the speed of an animal. Hooves still stir dust in the black loam beneath them; head and tail up, and forelegs leading her bulky frame as she eventually disappears into the woods.

"This cow is silly! Doesn't she see that she is bullying us with this strange behaviour?" I complain as we pierce through the trees, constantly bending low to lift the light branches that block our way, careful not to trip on broad tree roots protruding from the ground. Sometimes pricked by thorns, our eyes cast to the ground to see her footprints and avoid thistles, whose presence constantly announces itself to the soles of our bare feet, while our ears stay alert to hear the sound of her hooves touching the ground beneath them.

We ultimately leave the bush behind and sight Mvenyane trotting tiredly a short distance before us towards the Umzimvubu River. We follow her, walking on our painful shoeless feet and forcing forward our dog-tired bodies.

We are eager to know immediately what befell my father's herd or Mvenyane's calf that she did not come back with from the wild where they were driven together. My father's herd is his investment, which he proudly calls "My Bank!" His herd includes beasts with good mooing, beasts with finely shaped horns, and also those with unfamiliar, appreciable colours. These Ngunis provide our home with milk, meat, and hides that father sells to the skin traders in town. Also, their power in span pulls the sledge, the plough, the planter, and anything else behind them. And, too, their possession gives us males—boys and men—something to do; a responsibility to look after them, to care for them.

And, oh, how adorable Mvenyane's calf is! With round white spots on its tail, back, neck, head, face, and belly. Its prancing in the yard in the fashion of a hare in the wild graces our home extremely.

She follows the course of the river until she reaches a spot where she stops and solemnly lowers her head, bending her heavy neck, and sniffs at the ground with a loud beastly voice, the foamy saliva of strain from running dripping onto the ground from her heavy cupped lips.

We are just approaching that place as she suddenly moves away towards a certain tree on the outskirts of the bush we passed through. We do not mind her latter action and walk straight to the spot where she sniffed at the ground. We see fresh stains of blood. There are also blood traces pointing in the direction of Mvenyane. Mvenyane is now in the shade of the said tree, horning angrily at something under her nose, before her forelegs, horning it with an expression of extreme hate in her eyes and in all her appearance.

It is the carcass of a wild cat (a rare animal species in our region). The animal has bled profusely through wounds apparently caused by Mvenyane's sharp horns. The animal's needle-shaped long fangs and flappy tongue are still stained with the blood of something it has attacked and plundered or just injured.

Mvenyane's next move answers my question, "Why are Mvenyane's horns not painted with the blood of this wild animal if she killed it?" She starts pawing and poking the ground beneath her in a victorious mood. She even lows loudly in happiness; her horns are smeared with dust that has covered up or erased the evidence of her attack.

While we are still inspecting the red carcass of the wild cat with a short bushy tail, straight back, long pointed ears, eyes with black, white, and red rings, the catlike vigilant face, longish loose legs, and hunger-flattened white stomach, Mvenyane starts another move. She does not notice us in this move. She suddenly lifts her head and trots towards the river, towards the spot where she seemed to wait for us earlier.

On our arrival there, she immediately lowers her head and lows softly, kindly, apparently telling her first-born to stand up. It indeed starts standing up uneasily shaking and bleating quietly from the pinch of pain in the wound on its hind leg, from which blood still trickles down to the ground. Its mother is now standing aloof, apparently giving us a chance to perform our human duty of lifting her young one above the riverbank and carrying it home for healing and safekeeping. We wonder how it came to this perilous place—between the riverbank and a cluster of reeds whose roots are anchored in the sand under water.

At midday on our way back home, we meet our brothers (three young men who have been to mines and harbours) who have come to check if we are safe, having been away from home for quite a long time, and to know about the situation of my father's cattle in the veld considering Mvenyane's strange behaviour the previous morning. Our two pairs carry Mvenyane's injured calf and the carcass of the wild cat on their shoulders.

Mvenyane moves along peacefully; eyes pinned upon her calf, which one of our two pairs carries carefully on their shoulders. When we are nearing home, which is about a hundred metres away, Mvenyane puzzles us once again. She suddenly lifts her head and tail and takes a terrific run ahead of us, until she is in the yard. She then enters the kraal and starts doing something new. She paws the ground with the hoof of her right leg with great art and confidence. "Is she, by this move, thanking us for our positive response to her nonverbal report of the bad situation of her calf in the veld the previous morning?" I think aloud as we keenly watch the display.

8. To Register a Worker

We have had to register Mrs Nonzingo Njongo, whom at our home we call helper or aunt, not worker, to make her feel like one of us. The new labour law of the Republic of South Africa urges every home in the country to register its "domestic worker" with the Unemployment Insurance Fund (UIF) at the nearest office of the Department of Labour Affairs. Only two months remain before the deadline, and failure to do so warrants a heavy punishment.

Let me also say that, besides respecting the law of our land, there are other factors not to avoid the registration or cross the deadline. Certain complications arise that make it very difficult for us to act accordingly.

"Are you aware that what you are doing now can put this home in conflict with the law?"

"Yes, Bhuti, but my intention is not to do so. I know that by doing this I am neither honest with myself nor honourable to this home."

"When will you then enable us to register you and thus save this home from the wrath of the law, and save the home's dignity from waning because of our failure to act as we are expected?"

"When the time comes, I shall explain everything. Please just bear with me."

We are still wondering why this 45-year-old woman is failing to show us her newly obtained Identity Document so that we can register her – then she does the worst. She fails to return to work after she left to visit her children in her village, a distance away from Mthatha.

"Let us be careful, my husband. Let us look at this matter from both sides. This woman seems no longer interested in her work at this home, which also leads me to believe that she has left us to seek new employment."

"But don't you think that you are getting ahead of the situation by judging it?"

"I don't think so, but if that is the case, then it is because I am threatened and frustrated by Nonjongo's behaviour and her insensitivity to the urgency of this matter. May I also mention my fear about this strange behaviour of Nonjongo? I fear to say that this woman may have been hired by a cruel, jealous, and spiteful individual to harm your integrity as a devout and popular politician and councillor of this municipal ward and should be tarnished."

It is around the middle of the month when she suddenly appears at our doorstep, still prepared to wear her overall and bend over the broomstick. By now, we have already decided to sign her off and employ someone on a temporary basis in her stead. Our decision is not baseless at all. We did not receive a clear answer after we sent a person to her home in the tribal villages about 7 kilometres away to find out why she did not return to work. She had never behaved so irresponsibly before—only after we told her about our obligation to register her as a true and responsible employee.

"My child was sick. It was difficult for me to contact you and report my problem."

"When before did you have a similar problem and fail to report to us immediately?"

"Never before. Indeed, it was difficult for me to do so this time."

"Your ID, please!"

"Please bear with me. I am about to explain the complex situation to you."

"Are you aware that only a week remains before the deadline?"

"Yes. Please bear with me."

I too become suspicious and threatened by Nonzingo's strange behaviour. I feel unsettled inside as we sit around the table talking; she now tends to look away or above our heads or simply avoid eye contact as we speak. She has the talking eyes now—eyes that tell strange stories and have seemingly lost weight. Indeed, this light-complexioned and once weighty woman is no longer the person we are used to—the lady we have known and lived with for more than fifteen years.

After speaking to her, I find myself staring out through the kitchen window of our five-roomed brick and tiled home; yet, I am staring at nothing, although many things lie and move before me. I am seriously thinking of a way to find out what has changed the behaviour and ways of our Nonzingo. I am also trying to figure out if she is still interested in her work here at our home. Terror ticks through my heart and the marrow of my bones at the thought of the problem we may face if she dares to leave us. The results of her good service lie clear before our eyes and minds.

"And! Oh, the good care for our children! I recall the memories of how perfectly she looks after my children's safety and wellness, which she has done since they were babies with bibs and continued until they reached puberty. Let alone the role she plays in assisting them with their necessary education. Nonzingo never hesitates to report to us when our children are lazy about studying their school books or doing their homework. Nonzingo is actually their tutor, especially excelling in isiXhosa. Their home language is weakened by the syllabus of Private Schools, whose medium of education is mainly English, thus leaving less emphasis on our local traditional languages, which are the bearers of our African culture.

She also honourably assists in our obligation to teach them our cultural values that come from our great generations way back. She does so by telling them stories. We are greatly thankful for that because we have limited time and less knowledge to do so. One admired great value that she teaches them is Ubuntu.

That is not all! In fact, I can say with all respect that she is really one of us. Her service is not only to sweep with the broom or bend over the sink or scrub the bathtub. For the days when we are at work, on holidays far away, or gone to visit our village home 200 kilometres away, we entirely depend on her keen eyes and honest service. We have spent our sweet days and endured sour days together with her in this home.

My heart skips a beat from excitement on one particular Saturday morning as she says she needs to speak to us. I can only guess what she is going to say, so I quickly prepare my responses. "She will tell us that she intentionally gave us wrong information about her age, which we learned from her sister who once visited here at our home and gave us the correct information. She will tell us that she is secretly working chores at another home while employed by us, which we also suspect during our questioning and search for her strange behaviour." I think to myself, guessing incorrectly.

We sit around our dining table waiting patiently for quite a while, ready for the discussion with Nonzingo when she eventually leaves the kitchen to join us.
"Let me first apologise, Bhuti, and also to you, Sisi, for my delay in doing what you requested and reminded me to do. In fact, I am afraid to say that even today I am still not ready to do so, nor am I ready to explain why I cannot."
"What was the purpose of this meeting then, actually?"
"To discuss something else."
"Will that explain why you won't enable us to register you?"
"Perhaps, Bhuti. But that is not the purpose of this meeting."
"Please continue at once."
"My sole purpose in this meeting is to ask you, Bhuti, and you, Sisi, to accompany me to the local offices of the Department of Welfare, where I want to apply for a Disability Grant due to ill health."
"Are you ill? Seriously ill?"
"Yes, with arthritis, and it is serious."
"In short, you want to be relieved of your duties and would like us to accompany you to the local offices and assist you in applying for a Disability Grant?"
"Only to be accompanied to the offices."
"Why not both?"
"I shall explain that later."

A lot worse is yet to come from this! A lot more serious! I think to myself. Gratefully, the anger simmering within me because of what Nonzingo is doing quickly subsides and is replaced by panic about what I now suspect to be behind this unknown behaviour of this woman. I suspect that her illness is not caused by arthritis but something more serious.

There is more than just panic and frustration on the day I am at the Labour Department offices in Mthatha accompanying a member of my Constituency who has a labour problem. It is just excruciating pain. Employers of domestic workers from nearby suburbs, townships, and villages are all submitting their registration forms to avoid the deadline. Many employers are accompanied by their workers. The embarrassment to my soul when I have to mumble a reply to those wondering if I have already registered my worker is unbearable.

"Don't you think that she fears to say that she is entitled to higher wages?"

"Did she ever mention anything about it? Wasn't it only last month when she told us that only now helpers here in Mnqayi Street are earning wages equal to hers? Have you forgotten that? Nonzingo doesn't even fear to borrow money from us."

"What then do you suspect is behind all this?"

"Something more shocking, my wife."

"What is our next step then?"

"To call her to the table again and tell her that if she doesn't do as we ask, we shall have no other alternative but to end the contract between us. She will have no option but to stop her reluctance and postponements and give us a clear explanation there and then."

My wife's voice dries and dies in her throat as she calls Nonzingo from the kitchen for a final discussion about this matter in our small sitting room. Tutula becomes a new person as she tries to introduce the subject of the meeting. She stammers and swallows her words. She intends to speak out but cannot. So, I have to take over before the strain puts her to a stop or lowers her to the ground.

I understand the root cause of my wife's behaviour. She is also troubled by the same fear that troubles me, although I can endure the situation better. In fact, no one in our family, not even our youngest child, will behave normally realizing that we are about to part with Nonzingo. The evidence of her long, healthy, and honest service is inscribed on the walls of our hearts, and she has succeeded in proving herself to be one of us.

She once told us about her pathetic background in the village of Sibangweni. Sibangweni is a village in the district of Libode. We know she left school at the young age of 14 while still doing only Standard 8, as a punishment by her parents after falling pregnant. She then got married at the tender age of 16. Her husband died shortly while working at the coal mines in KwaZulu-Natal when she was 26 years old, leaving her with their four children to care for.

She was then forced for the first time to be the breadwinner at her home. We also understand that before we employed her, she was selling firewood that she cut and collected from young trees on municipal land on the banks of the Mthatha River, and she and others were constantly arrested by the police, as that act was illegal and disallowed by the by-laws of our local municipality.

My dear wife makes one last motherly attempt to settle and talk to Nonzingo privately about this sensitive matter. As a woman, she feels that maybe she can bring up this issue by discussing it quietly with Nonzingo in her lonely room at the back of our home.

Tutula steps down from our back door and walks to Nonzingo's room, still unsure what to say or ask. We both know that we need and want to register this woman, as we both realize the urgency of this matter.

Nonzingo simply uses a new stubborn strategy in her resistance to honour our request. Now she shows extreme submissiveness while my wife tries to talk to her safely.

Nonzingo only sits there in silence, rolling her eyes while tears set upon them. My wife's attempt, as woman to woman—rather than master and servant—turns sour. Actually, the conversation fails and ends before it even starts.

"The position of any woman is weakened further by unemployment. Therefore, never allow any situation that can subject you to unemployment." This is one of the things Tutula says to Nonzingo, getting no response.
"Only two days are left before the Department closes all registrations and sends out Inspectors to check if all homes

have complied with this new act. Also, we can't afford to always fear the long arm of the law each time we see a person who resembles a Labour Department officer approaching our home.

"Your reluctance to give us a copy of your ID and your refusal to explain why you behave this way lays great strain on our souls. Our children also seem to have noticed this awkward situation in our home, and we are unable to explain to them the cause. Hence, we have decided to ask you again, and you now have one last chance to explain, as you have always promised to do."

"It is only fear, Bhuti, and towards you, Sisi! My fear of losing this job that has served me and my children for the past 15 years, and the fear of turning my back on the people who have been like family to me. This fear developed during an evening debate on the Unitra Community Radio about the new labour laws. The debate revealed that these laws shall not positively affect us, the domestic workers, although their primary objective is to protect and serve us better. The debate further revealed that we shall lose our jobs because most employers cannot afford to pay workers the set minimum wage of R800.00 a month. That night I slept only with my eyes, not my mind nor my heart. That is when I decided never to allow this situation to happen to me by blocking the signing of the form and not handing over a copy of my ID to you."
"Have you lost confidence in our traditional way of solving problems in this home? In the past, we always used to meet around the table and discuss any problem or matter of the day."

"No, Bhuti. But this time, the fear was too heavy to bear and too worrisome."

We only stare at each other in amazement and silence, looking at her appearance and listening as she continues: "Let me also reveal to you that I am already dead. I am a ghost walking on the face of this earth. I died along with my friends and my foes in this suburb after we were told by our employers to lay down our brooms upon the announcement of this new law! Their madams told them that they couldn't afford to keep them in the kitchens because of the new high wages to pay for their sweat."

"But you surely are aware by now that our home's private matters always start around this table and end around this table. You know that."

"I say I am a ghost! There is no reason to wear the overall again if soon I shall have to undress it. I am a ghost!"

9. A New Home

My family and other people in Mhlotsheni village do not only dislike my purchasing a house in the city by a mortgage bond, but they dislike everything about it. And it seems I don't have sufficient energy to change them.

"Now ma, you have a place in the city of Mthatha where you can visit when you want to refresh yourself or see specialist doctors," I say to my beloved mother, Mary-Jane Nondima MaRhadebe Mlandu, expecting to see ripples of a smile on her slightly wrinkled dark face, stimulated by the news of my great achievement. But this doesn't happen.

Instead, she wants me to explain this and explain that even before we start seriously discussing the matter. "It is not easy for me even to understand you when you say you purchased a home on credit. I only know home as a very significant commodity which ought not to be purchased with a condition that it can revert back to the original owner who will sell it to somebody else should the buyer fail to pay back their money plus profit in the form of instalments. I know a home as a commodity that gives shelter and address to the members; provides space for their family bonding activities; and as where a member can turn their heart inside out when they experience joy or bitterness. Not as something that is obtained but with an apparent risk of loss," she says looking at me in amazement.

My mention and explanation of the word "mortgage bond" has her clapping her hands. "Who taught you that, my son?"

"Nobody but the situation, ma."

"What situation, my beloved son?"

"The need to have a house while I have insufficient money to buy it in cash."

"Do you earn stones, not money, at the end of the month?"

"The money I earn is so small that it does not enable me to buy a house at full price. And to save money for this deal can thus take me numerous years while I need my personally owned accommodation now."

"Do you then really regard that house as yours even with its dual ownership?"

"Oh, yes, mama! And I feel proud of it." She then keeps quiet and only looks at me with eyes weighted with unasked questions.

"Also, ma, my stay at Ngangelizwe Township where I enjoyed paying low rental has, after my marriage and having children, become a problem as the rented rooms there are so small for a family man like me. And shifting to the suburbs such as Ikhwezi, Norwood and Ncambedlana (especially the last two) too had a snag of high rental which was a little more than the monthly instalment that I am paying towards my account at the bank for my new home. Which means if I went there, I would just be delaying my personal development in this regard," I add.

Throughout this visit, I am unable to enjoy the homeliness of my home. And each conversation we have always leads to the same topic. "Do you mean that you have now forgotten what you ought not to have forgotten, Soga my son?"

"Will you please come clear on that, ma?"

"I mean the appreciable role that you have always played towards the development and happiness of this home with your monthly financial assistance."

"If you mean that, I can safely say that there shall be no change at all, my dear mother. Of course, with a great strain as I also have to maintain my young family – the wife and two children." "I pity you, my child, as I clearly see the strain that will be laid on you by the bank. They will always stretch their hand to receive back their money from you with no patience but a threat of snatching back their commodity if you fail to pay your instalment even for one month. I pity you." Looking at me from behind her heavy-lensed spectacles, my mother says.

Beside my deeply rooted love for my mother, my only mother, I am aware that being peasants, my parents, herself and my late father Jacob Msebenzi Mlandu, had not qualified for pension insurance although they could pay premiums, and that the number of their livestock that had supported them with income from their sales and sales of their skins and wool to the traders had now shrunk drastically. Hence, I don't wonder when she wants to know about continuation or discontinuation of my financial assistance to my village home.

And I sense that the news of my latest move has quickly crossed rivers and reached many ears in places away from Mhlotsheni village. This becomes clear during my surprise visit at the place of my uncle who stays some kilometres away from my village. It does not take long during our conversation before he twists our talk and cleverly leads it straight to the common topic of the weekend. "…Let me first tell you this, my brother's son, that I knew the city and its ill tendencies long before you were born. In the city, especially in the suburb where I worked as a gardener, neighbours are neighbours only physically – spiritually they are placed far apart. One may even be tempted to say that the fence does not only divide their yards but also their hearts. It is only among us, your tribesmen here in the village, that you live among those who care about you and your existence and your safety. Let alone the complexities and expensiveness of the city," the man in his early seventies says, but I don't answer him. Instead, I keep on nodding positively, respectfully. I do not want to reveal my strong feeling, or rather my determination about my action to him.

Another act of dislike is yet to be encountered. I suspected this when this morning I received an invitation from Chief Ziphathe Ndumiso Sontsi of Mhlotsheni Village, my village, who urgently wants to see me at his royal place. I even deliberate about it within me as I walk to the Great Place with the lightest foot. "…This act of yours causes me some fears, fears of a serious situation, where this village may simply become empty of its young blood and of hope for a better future. This loss of its first son whom we gave better education tells me that the city is cleverer than the village. The city educates its youth who then uplift it while the village educates its youth who then turn their backs on it to go and uplift the city which already has a lot of uplifters." He then pauses and pulls hard on his long beaded wooden pipe; his sadness reflecting on his old face.

He immediately changes the topic on seeing the change in my facial expression and my general mood. There is a drizzle of tears on my face and a lump in my throat. Two things are paining me deeply: his speech and my knowledge of why he talks like this.

Except for being a chief that cares most for the general development of his village and his subjects who include parents and children, Chief Sontsi always shows a unique sentiment towards my home, which I believe is caused by the fact that his grandfather Chief Jani Sontsi and my grandfather Mr Ellias Rhashula Mlandu participated together in the First World War, and my father has always been one of the senior councillors at the Royal House. As well as I am among the few youth members who have obtained better academic education and have had exposure to city life while showing keen interest in general affairs of the village.

I honestly respect our Tribal Chief for his love for education and his tireless struggle for the general development of our village. The school where I first encountered the teacher, its construction had been funded with the money he and his committee had collected from his subjects. And in the gatherings where he addresses the youth, he does not forget to say the words that I respect most, "Your shield, your spear, is the pen," and concludes with the words, "We educate you and discipline you so that you can preserve and expand the values of this great village." His speech during our conversation reminds me of these words and touches my soul.

My great pity is that these people don't know how strongly I am attached to Mhlotsheni despite my latest move. Mhlotsheni, my birthplace, the place where my umbilical cord fell, where my kin and age-mates live, where the bones of my forbears lie underneath, and where I first encountered the world and its complications interpreted for me. I know that they don't know how proud I am to belong to that tribal village, despite its economic stagnation, cultural boredom and belatedness compared to the city of Mthatha. They don't know that the more I fade into the distance from it, the more its voice becomes louder and clearer in my inward ears. They don't know this.

It is before we are parted and my spiritual disturbance having disappeared when Chief Sontsi concludes his speech. "When we see our youth receive better education and get exposed to the knowledge of the city, we simply hope that they will use that power in canvassing for this place facilities that make the city attractive to rural elites and its prospective guests overseas and most valuable and enjoyable to its dwellers. We then get disappointed when our youth don't do that but instead depart from it to use that power in developing the already developed urban areas."

My purchasing a house in the city was influenced by a number of factors. First, I wanted to get my own residential accommodation. Being a tenant in Ngangelizwe Township, where I rented a room, had many challenges for me. In Ngangelizwe I actually didn't need somebody or something to remind me that my home was actually in the villages on the other side of the far away mountains – 130 kilometres away. The behaviour of some of the stand-owners, and sometimes also their children, was there to do this. I encountered this on my first day in the first yard: as I was notified of the rules that were there to be obeyed by the dwellers of that yard. "Visitors are reported! Never keep visitors here! The gates are locked at 8pm!" And I later found out that these rules were the same in all the yards of the great township. To get my room, I had been forced to do what other desperate accommodation seekers did. I started paying rental while the mud and brick flat that I had identified to occupy was still under construction.

Second, some of the landowners, especially the females, brewed umqombothi (the African corn beer) and sold it to the tenants and visitors – this happening throughout the seven days of the week and across lengthy nights of the weekends. It was often accompanied by selling marijuana and very dangerous drugs. And these resulted in common occurrence of loud shouts and bloody fights amid deafening music from the blaring hi-fis and screams of the night girls. So unbearable to me during my study time furthering my education or when lifting the pen to produce a manuscript or just reading for pleasure.

Their children – I mean those who were troublesome – would outsize the stand-owners in their ways of troubling the tenants that I was one of them. In one yard, myself and two others who were my friends and who had found me accommodation there, suffered from a different kind of hardship which happened each night of the pay day. The two sons of our landlord and a group of their friends would return from the liquor places in the dead of the night: singing songs of many kinds of music at the same time and in an uncoordinated fashion. We would identify them with that noise and come together in one rented room to receive them with our certain type of kindness, which protected us from the nuisance that they always made. We collected small monies and offered them on their arrival at the room so that they didn't stay but went back to where they came from and perhaps also slept there, lowered to the floor by the influence of more liquor.

Their arrival on the yard was announced by their body-banging on the doors. Having them inside meant that we did nothing else but listen to the loud uncoordinated music and see them falling into a pile-up on the floor causing us a burden of lifting them up and carrying them to their respective rooms for sleep.

Let me not forget to state that there were also those landlords and landladies that, because of their kindness, we found ourselves compelled to call them tata or mama instead of master or madam. In them we found the parents that we had left home, beyond the horizon. One of such people would even call an ambulance and pay it out of her own pocket, to be refunded later, if one of us fell sick while he had no money to go to the hospital as those days no one throughout South Africa entered into the hospital and got medication without pay. Their spirit of Ubuntu!

By leaving Ngangelizwe for Northcrest, I was really not running away from these problems. No. I only wanted to have my own place in the city. And I was not blindfolded to the cultural losses which I would sustain by leaving the great township which had been the home and meeting place for black people and being upholder of the values of African humanity, Ubuntu. Ngangelizwe was and still is known as the entry point into the city of Mthatha for the people from the villages like myself then.

I repeat, nothing seems to stop the dislike of these people who don't approve of my purchasing a house in the city. Reading from their whispered verbal expressions, I establish another factor. I gather that they see my latest move only as an act of an African who is departing from his village to join the white man in the city and looking down upon his black community and their ways in the village because of possession of better school education. "School education is not good and it doesn't favour us if it makes its holder look down upon his own people and their place of residence and leave to join the traditional dwellers of the city, the whites," one of them explodes after our greetings, before he tries by all kinds of ways to influence me to withdraw from my move.

In my humble response, I explain that city life is not meant for people of a particular race and that people of other races in the city could as well come to settle in the village if they so wish. Explaining that the impression that they hold in this regard has actually been created by the influence of racial laws and racial practices whose time has but come to an end.

And I have tried all possible ways to convince these people that my purchasing a house in the city makes no difference in my attitude and commitment towards my village. I also explained that this is why I did not stop my financial support and regular visits to my home, and my attendance to the events of my clan of amaBhele and to those of the community of Mhlotsheni.

"Soga my son, the weight of old age accompanied by illness feels too heavy on me now; and I realise that not long I will join your father in the cold bed beneath the surface of the earth, there in the corner of our garden. It will therefore be a pity if that moment comes while you are away from us. And let me explain further that, when we enabled you to get the better school education, we were not helping you alone, but also ourselves. To be straight to the point, I must state that we were arming you to be able to fend for yourself in adulthood and also to keep our good name ranking high in this community of Mhlotsheni — as parents of a better-educated child. So, your departure from here virtually works against our objectives," my mother says looking at me with hardly blinking eyes behind her heavy-lensed spectacles.

I am still thinking about this talk when I receive a message from the Village Chief which has been brought to my home by one of the Great One's councillors. And when I arrive there, the Great One nearly introduces his subject during our greetings. "The land which is currently allocated for housing is now getting finished, and it will take the village too long to have one of the lands now allocated for grazing converted into housing land."

I nod continuously, positively, respectfully, as he speaks. And after appreciating the offer, I inform the Great One that my elder sister has found me a land in our great village of Mhlotsheni with a house on it from somebody who is selling it, preparing to emigrate to another village which lies next to the National Road and closer to the town of Mount Frere. Unmoved, I conclude that we are still going to approach the Great One for his recommendation for change of ownership of the affected property. "I will willingly recommend the change of ownership of the land from the original owner to you to the District Magistrate's office," he concludes our talk with waves of a smile of appreciation traveling across his oldish ebony face.

My mother's younger sister, Sis Ntsiki, sings sweetly and dances with dexterity amid ululations from attendants at the home-opening ceremony when she says, "He is a man of two worlds, the city and the village. Better that than a total departure." I see the half-confidence in the faces of the guests, and understand them; and also feel satisfied.

10. It Glitters Behind the Bars

Sigqebhezana and the other young women in khaki dresses cleaning long passages are unaware that someone overhears their conversation. I mean someone in the highest chair of this institution.

"Now I am going to do it in the faraway towns."

"Do what?"

"Steal articles from the shops and hide them between my thighs."

"So that you come back to this punishment?"

"Better that than what I have to endure there, outside."

It was after overhearing this conversation that the authorities of a prison in Western Pondoland decided to call back the NGO I head to conduct another workshop and assist them in changing Sigqebhezana's behaviour, which lands her in jail so often and risks her life. Actually, the name Sigqebhezana is not the real name of this sixteen-year-old girl. The name means mini-skirt. Sigqebhezana got the name on her first stay in this prison because she wore the smallest skirt and was the youngest female prisoner.

This is now the third time that Sigqebhezana is serving a penalty in this prison. Only during her first days inside was she haunted by prison. "But, oh, the stubborn walls! The constant rattle of keys when they come to count us, even in the dead of night!" she exclaimed when we interviewed her.

Another thing that Sigqebhezana hates in prison is the harassment from the male prisoners when they see her in her mini-skirt. They whistle, clear their throats loudly and repeatedly, and swallow fake saliva noisily. She then thinks they do this simply because she is the youngest female here, and cries until others comfort her.

From the second time of shoplifting and consequent imprisonment, Sigqebhezana no longer cared about the hardships in prison – the hands of her detainers in shops, and the bondage of isolation inside the prison cells. She has become used to the hard hands of her detainers as they land on her flesh and to their tongues as they sting her with questions. In fact, Sigqebhezana now regards the prison walls as her other home.

The story of her life is visible on her body. Her once beautiful face is marred by a scar running across her left cheek. Sigqebhezana got the scar while trying to escape from workers of a supermarket in Mthatha and falling over a sharp object.

And indeed, she is correct when she says she has to endure a lot of hardship in the freedom outside the prison, particularly in her home. When we interview her mother, who is carrying Sigqebhezana's child on her back and sitting on the grass mat spread on the cow dung-carpeted floor next to their single bed, she says: "Sigqebhezana is our daughter. She left her home because its fireplace is always cold."

"Our daughter doesn't listen to us, perhaps because we are poor. Please help us to change her bad behaviour," her father, who digs and sells river sand to individuals and contractors, adds.

Certainly, this family wouldn't be in this bad situation if Sigqebhezana's father had still been employed in the gold mines of Johannesburg, from where he had always sent home registered envelopes. He might have still been in that city if they hadn't had the child after a long time of waiting and battling. Hence, his wife did what none of them had wished for: she left the village home for the city to see specialist doctors and stayed there for a while.

Sigqebhezana's father didn't remain in Johannesburg but returned with his family to the Transkei to work near them and his property. The decision to quit his job in the gold mines was not difficult. He was not worried about money or the prospects of a hard life with low-paying jobs in the rural village in the Transkei.

Although Sigqebhezana can read and write, she has never seen the face of the blackboard. The little she knows, she learnt from her peers. She was twelve when she lost her girlhood, and fourteen when she gave birth to a baby. She resorted to stealing after her life of cohabitation with the father of her child failed. She tells us why she had to leave the young man: "I had grown too big to depend on someone else for living. Let alone that my boyfriend also treated me like his wife although he had not paid even a penny for lobola (bride price), and was restricting me from working while I had to support my family."

When Sigqebhezana finally left her home, she went to live on the streets. Her boyfriend had met her there, smelling of spirits, covered with cardboard sheets at night for a blanket. Street life gave her knowledge and experience of things she had not known happened to people, things that happened to street kids! Things like these: that it is useless to cry for help when in trouble in the dead of night because no help exists for you; that there is nowhere to run when troubled at this time, as wherever you arrive you are regarded as the troublemaker; and that in the morning not only girls in the street groan from the pains of rape, but the boys too. She narrated this to us in one interview.

Her decision followed a hard time for her and her home; she was mature already when this happened. She saw the heavy rains that fell for some days in our region. She was among the escapees when floods broke and drove away the mud-and-stick settlement formed by their homes in the Ncambedlana Valley. She also saw her father, who steadfastly followed the course of the stream for a week searching for possible remnants of his animals—the fowls, goats, and sheep that he had brought from the village—as he returned with tardy, tired feet, his hands clasped together behind him hopelessly.

During their brief stay in the tent on the yard of the Ncambedlana Methodist Church, Sigqebhezana developed a strange feeling—anger and hate. She hated everybody: the other refugees, the caregivers, her parents, and herself. "It was very hard for me to accept that awkward situation, that life of dependence and hopelessness. I also felt terrible displeasure and hate when I saw my parents cup their hands and bend their knees, receiving grants from 'the other men and women' who worked for the Red Cross and government agencies."

Her job at a madam's kitchen ended on bad advice from one of her friends in the streets. "Why do you break your tender body behind the broom and over the bathtub while there is a far easier way of getting money?"
"What do you mean?"
"I mean to live by your wits and be able to go home every day with a heavy bag of money."

Perhaps it is these things and others that now make Sigqebhezana unwilling to be interviewed. Expressing her unwillingness, she says: "The history of my problem is long—our time is short." And says, "Talking of this problem tortures me and weakens me." Or else says, "I lack good words to enable me to come clear on it."

"Sigqebhezana has chosen to live a fast life, empty of responsibilities." This is said by my colleague after our team's visit to Sigqebhezana's home. Sigqebhezana finishes her prison term but instead of coming back home, returns to her old life in the streets.

Her parents don't rest when she fails to pitch up. They do a ceaseless search. "It worries us greatly to see her baby boy grow up in our care but in the absence of his mother with whom he is going to live after we have been absorbed by the ground," her mother says within herself during their continuous search. She repeats this in one of our visits to their shack.

A few days after all these events, I open my correspondence and find a letter signed by Sigqebhezana. The letter says: "Sir, please find me a job and accommodation at the night school. Very soon I will be at your office."

11. But, oh, the Sea!

Grandmother Mazombane Bhaza is surprisingly healthy and strong today, on this day of her request. "My problem can be solved if I can be transported to the seaside. Just the touch of the sea breeze on me, the smell of the salty waters in my nose, the sight of the transient hills, the sight of the playful seals, and the soft screeches of the seagulls."

She defeats us when we try to stop her from standing for a long time as she speaks to us, and from moving around the room without the support of her walking stick, her hands clasped together behind her. We are honestly against anything that can lay a strain on our 87-year-old grandmother.

Grandmother bursts out, "The sea is medicine. The coolness of its breeze will touch me tenderly, travel nicely through my aged body—tickling every sinew in me, and fill the marrow in my bones with solace. Please, take me to the sea!"

She ordered my uncle Zadoyi to convene the meeting in which she is speaking. Sitting in her chair, leaning forward on her walking stick, her eyes cast on each and every one of us in the large room of her six-cornered mud and thatch house.

It is really painful to see how old age and sickness have robbed her of her weight and strength and blunted her sweet soprano voice, leaving only her wits and her sense of hearing.

Can we, members of her family, easily nod positively to her request? The answer is no. "My mother's personal doctor shall be approached to approve any step that we take honouring mama's request," my uncle Zadoyi suggests with respect and humility. "The doctor is an outsider to this matter. Practically an outsider! Hence, I did not instruct you to invite him to this meeting," grandmother scolds my uncle, and for some time we are all tense. Grandmother is aware of the power of her authority over us. And it feels good to respect it.

The distance of approximately 215 kilometers that exists between my grandma's village of Rhode in the district of Mount Ayliff and the beaches of Port St Johns, which is the nearest, is great and crushing for grandmother's ailing health condition. And too, about 35 kilometers of this distance is still gravel road, with discomforting turns and bends, especially below the Mlengana rocks where it also slopes.

"We really lack words to tell how much we love you, grandmother. And we all know that there is no one on this vast, wide earth who can replace you if we happen to lose you. And we will regret throughout our lives having lost you because of our carelessness. What I want to say to you, grandma, is that the distance and the condition of the road to be travelled through on our planned journey shall be strenuous and dangerous for your ill health," one of us pleads, her hands clasped together on her breast and bending her knees so often as if grandmother sees her clearly. "The sea is medicine, my grandchild. It will cure even the effects of that. Take me to the sea!" she responds. And I sense a strain in her voice and hear whistles in her breathing pulse, and pity her extensively.

We are really not strong enough while we rehearse the songs and dances that we are going to perform on the beach when we entertain her. Grandmother's continuously worsening condition is worrisome to us. And there is still no change in her health when the date and time for our departure arrive. We even forget to buy the presents that we planned to purchase for her.

Grandmother still refuses all kinds of food that we offer her when the minibus arrives at her place to transport us to the coast. This problem forces one of us to plead with grandma for postponement of the trip, and we apologize to the transport owner. "The sea does wonders. Perhaps your teachers did not tell you this. And I have told you some of the ingredients that the sea uses to heal the ills of the people. And, oh, the gagged rumbles of its white-capped gambolling hills! And their spasmodic splashes against the rocks, and their swashes and purrs as they return to where they came from. Please take me to the sea!" she says confidently and with more determination.

Grandmother grew up in the villages in the southern parts of what is now Eastern Cape, villages that lay not very far from the coastal city of East London. And she had already married Reverend Joseph Bhaza, my maternal grandfather, when they emigrated together inland, spreading Christianity under the auspices of the Ethiopian Church. Her Standard Five education strongly enabled her to establish and run an academic school within each church mission that they had established and occupied. And each church mission also had an appendage in the form of an orchard that they established together. Even now, grandmother still loves to be called Titshalakazi (Lady Teacher). Throughout their life together, Titshalakazi and Reverend Bhaza (her husband who has now passed on) were no strangers to the seaside; they always visited there using hired cars or riding grandpa's horses.

"We are about to land at the beach! We shall be welcomed by constant bangs of huge waves!" We are still many kilometers away from the sea when grandmother says this. Surprisingly, when we arrive at the beach, we are indeed welcomed by the bangs of vigorous waves. Good guess!

With a revived strong voice, she also asks us to add cushions to her seat. The cushions are actually to add to the blankets and scarves that grandmother is already wreathed within, and also two woollen hats that she is wearing on her head. We even stand up and crowd the passage of the minibus to peer over her, excited by the noticeable improvement in the strength of grandmother's voice.

We do that until she asks us to leave her alone, saying what is hard for us, her children, to discern. "Please allow me to communicate with myself. And I am already connected to the sea." I think drowsiness has interfered with grandmother's brainpower.

"We have arrived at the place where the sea comes urgently to meet people, to play with people, to heal the ills of the people. Here, for once, people become one—whapped together by the furious wave, which but loves to hear the laughter," she concludes.

Our tenacious attention to grandma denies us the opportunity to join the half-naked multitudes of people who throng both First Beach and Second Beach—shuffling through the white warm succumbing sand, picking up and playing with shells, taking photos of each other lying on their backs on the warm black shining rocks, or lazing in the cool under the shade of their umbrellas.

We sing and dance for grandmother until she stops us. Now the sun is already hanging too low over the blue plains of waters far away there and here where waters are surging and surfing at their edges.

"I shall come back here only to glance at the lighthouse. I have loved the service it renders for the ships. I have rendered similar service for my children and for the children of my children," she says. And we look at her with all the respect, and cry tears that are nothing else but a certificate of honour for her.

12. Honey

Our search for honey happens in a specific way and in a specific manner.

In Mlotsheni Village, we conduct the search in the morning or afternoon of a clear day: at such times and on such days, movements of the bees in the sky around or above their nest are exposed, making it easy for us to locate their nest. We know that cloudiness can blur our view and spoil our search.

We do not conduct the search on a cold, windy, or rainy day; on such days, bees do not risk their health and safety by setting off to find nectar and pollen with which they build honey. Instead, they stay inside their residence and feed on the wealth they have accumulated. This is confirmed by the isiXhosa proverb which says: Iinyosi zibenza zibutya ubusi – Bees gather honey not only to keep it but also to find food in it. The meaning is that people must enjoy the fruits of their labour.

There are signs that indicate to us the existence of a bee-nest at a particular place, which we always look out for immediately upon our arrival at a place where we are to conduct the search. The common appearance of some kinds of mice, some kinds of birds—particularly that small grey bird called the honey bird—the serpents, and other honey-eating creatures, especially if they appear in numbers, attracts our attention and encourages us to intensify our search until we locate the bees' wealth. We also analyze the direction of the movement of these creatures, which always points to the location of the bee-nest, assisting us in discovery.

The honey bird does not only indicate the existence of the hive there, it also leads us straight to it, expecting to have a share or to pick up crumbs after our harvesting. Screaming softly and beating its wings artistically in the air above us, it hovers over the location of the bee-nest and stops when it sees us heading for the place with the bee-hive, to witness the harvesting and wait for its share from a small distance.

Through much aggression, the bees of the nest with honey signal to us the existence of their nest in the place where we have come to conduct the search. They attack anyone and anything that appears to move toward their settlement. This aggression also indicates the hugeness of their wealth in that residence, which is explained by the isiXhosa proverb: Iinyosi zingasuzela zityebile – Only bees with honey sting.

The hunter or ordinary traveler who has unfortunately fallen under the attack of these aggressors is not rescued from hardship even by running away or lying down hoping they will stop their attack and leave him. While running, the bees continue their attack, planting their stings in his head, face, and neck. Lying down does not help either, as a small cloud of bees keeps on buzzing above him, while some individuals fly down to crawl all over his body searching for a bare spot to sting. Their stings remain in his flesh to inject poison which causes swelling in and around the affected area.

Goats and wild buck behave strangely when attacked by bees. They come together bewildered and stamp the ground uneasily, then run away prancing about in pain or even bleating. The aggressors chase these animals until they are far from their settlement.

Instead of discouraging us, this behaviour of the bees encourages us to intensify our search for honey in that specific geographic location. We know that on the other side of the bees' stings is honey.

These are not the only signals indicating the existence of the bee-nest nearby. Even their buzz, as bees are a singing kind of creature, invites us to where their nest is. We are also able to pick up the smell of honey among the sweet scents that permeate the neighborhood of the hive. We follow the direction of the honey smell until we reach the waxed doorway of the hive.

Other things also assist our search. An example is the uniqueness of the structure of a bee's body and the uniqueness of the movement of bees around their nest.

Appearing in the sky, the brown hairy bodies of the bees and their roundish yellow and transparent papery wings make them such a unique set of insects in the sky, especially when they are reflected by the soft rays of the morning or afternoon sun.

The movement of the bees flying around the swarm's residence with the intention of spying on and attacking enemies or prospective enemies is vastly different from the movements of other insects commonly seen in the sky. The movement aims not only at protecting the wealth inside their residence but also to protect the queen bee, who is a highly treasured figure, and other members such as egg-layers, the aged, the sick, and the maggots. These movements catch our eyes and lead us to a happy discovery.

We have been told and ourselves continuously observe the cleverness of the bees in how they behave to avoid identification of their nest. One of their tricks is that when they return from hunting for nectar and pollen, some bees do not fly straight to the residence but, while still at a considerable distance, fly down to the ground and reach their nest crawling to elude possible observers. This act is confirmed by the greasy traces found on the bees' tracks. Their singular movements when they leave the nest to search for nectar and pollen and when they return are associated not only with their attempt to avoid delays on their forays but also with avoiding identification of their nest by enemies, including ourselves, the searchers.

Swarms settle and create honey in different locations such as holes in donga walls or riverbanks dug by mice creating their dwellings; in holes of ant-heaps dug by ant-eaters—some wild animals—and those at the base of some tree trunks caused by rotting, crumbling, and wasting away, leaving room for a swarm to settle and create honey.

The swarm usually leaves its residence for another suitable place after we have harvested their treasure, especially if we did not leave any of it or if we used smoke to drive or drug the swarm aside before harvesting. We suspect that the bees identify and earmark the alternative residence while searching for nectar and pollen away from their current residence.

We also know there are sites vacated by the swarm after harvesting or heavy plundering but, after some time, we find them harboring a swarm again. We are not sure if the swarm we find at the affected venue is the one that left after the previous exploitation or a totally new swarm. These sites are notable for their concrete structure and warmth for the swarm. They are commonly located in rocky places.

There are also sites in which the bees live permanently. In isiXhosa, the swarm that does not leave its residence even after a series of harvesting incidents is called itsili. The itsili has the following characteristics:

Its residence is found in a perilous place like the face of a cliff. The interior of its residence is lavishly roomy, hence the harvest is never exhausted; and the swarm has the most aggressive and vigilant members.

When I reached my hunting age, my paternal grandfather, Ellias Rhashula Mlandu (1877–1964), led me by hand to one of the sites in our village which harbored the itsili. It is among the rocks in the place called IliwaLangaseDiphini – The rocks near the local Dipping Tank. He told me that while he was a boy, he and other boys harvested honey there an incalculable number of times, which neither made the swarm depart nor their harvest get depleted.

As mentioned earlier, we do not conduct the search haphazardly: we rely entirely on gazing, shielding our eyes with our hands to spot the residence of the bees with honey. We move in a row to cover the targeted area or scan the affected area standing at its lower part and gazing—starting from its uppermost region to its lowermost region. Among us, we always have some excellent gazers.

A discovery! We are always sure to make a discovery. Surely, because ours is a honey belt: a honey belt due to having a variety of aloes whose flowering supplies bees with the nectar and pollen they need to construct honey. This condition is confirmed by the names of some tribal villages in the Eastern Cape, such as Nyosini, Manyosini, Zinyosini, and KwaNyosi. All these names mean "at the bees," or "at the home of bees."

The swarm will be seething, surging, and buzzing all over and about its harvest or will have moved aside when we start our exploitation to fill our small buckets with the brown, yellow, and white slices of honey, our mouths already watering.

13. Lamb's Bleats

When I find the two sheep I was looking for, I have already traveled up many hills, descended many slopes, and crossed many plains near Mhlotsheni Village, my village. I find them at the scene of disaster.

What led me to where I and the two sheep are—here on the flat land, near a rivulet, below a hillock—was the lamb's incessant bleat. The lamb was nervously grazing around the breathless body of its mother, which lay limp on the grass-covered land.

Hastening to come close to the dead body of the ewe to inspect it and find out the cause of her death, I am stopped by the lamb's bleat. The bleat is pitiful and yet protesting.

My second attempt, too, is unsuccessful. The lamb does not only bleat; it also runs challengingly around the dead body of its mother. Hence, I pause for a moment to study the strange behavior of this young animal, searching for a solution to my problem.

Like those before it, my other attempt—to chase and catch the lamb so I can go home with it—fails. This time the lamb speeds away even towards dangerous places like pools and dongas. Fearing for its safety, I stop the chase.

Apparently, the lamb refuses to subject itself to any situation that could make it lose sight of the body of its beloved mother; it is not discouraged by the mother's inactivity or the clumsy way she lies on the ground.

It seems unaware that I am trying to help it, nor aware that it is not the only one troubled inside by the current state of affairs of its mother; as we at home now have a minus against the number of our flock.

My worry! I am worried for the health of this lamb as it continuously sucks milk from the teats of the dead ewe. Which may have been killed by snake poison. This poison may have been carried through the ewe's body by circulating blood and reached the udder and teats before she died.

When it bleats, the desperate lamb stretches its neck, hunches its back, and flattens its belly. Bleating with a coarse voice, it scarcely nibbles on spring grass.

Its bleat is actually the cry of a baby who does not want to be separated from her mother.
At home, we do what we always do in such circumstances. We feed this particular lamb from a bottle of powdered milk or make it suckle at the teats of other ewes.

It now dawns on me that my necessary task is to convince the lamb that its mother is dead; therefore, she cannot stand up again, offer warm milk, or welcome it with motherly body movements; nor will they lie side by side on their bellies and chew cud simultaneously again. But how can I do this? The question remains unanswered.

When I prepare to stand up from the log where I have been sitting for a while, to chase the lamb now from the side of the pools and dongas—ensuring its safety when I do this— the disaster completes its cycle. And the lamb bleats once more as danger hovers over it, over both of us. The sudden fall of the shadow of a cloud of vultures lowering over us from the clear sky above signals their voracious visit to the carcass of the ewe.

The bleat is clearly the lamb's shout against the invaders so they do not land near its place of hope. I whistle softly as the strong-built, huge-bodied birds land near their target and start tearing it apart, making it a has-been in no time.

I am really not sure if the last bleat from the lamb's throat was already quiet in the air when I observe the lamb's absence where it was—among the hoarding things. I strongly wield my stick to remind the birds of my superior power, man's superior power, as they scour madly for something else to prey on.

I then leave the place that has suddenly become silent.

14. Blood Bond

The bond of blood relationship between my 13-year-old nephew, Sibongiseni Lutho, and myself is today strongly tested. I contribute by reacting with anger. Worst of all, this nearly makes me forget his dismal background in the township in Ngangelizwe, and cease my plans of pulling him out of his troubles and protecting him from further hazards.

The school holiday he is spending with us in Northcrest on my traditional invitation has not yet ended when he does something that makes me chase him off and tell him never to return. I see his eyes drowning in tears. His head hangs in shame over his chest and his voice suffocates in grief. He pleads for mercy and promises he will never misbehave again. I am not moved. Something rages within my breast. I remain looking at him with raging fire in my eyes and point him to the gate. I just seal my ears with wax as my children beg me to pardon Sibongiseni and let him stay with us until the end of the holiday. I then accompany him across the lawn to the gate.

"How many times have I warned you about your violent behavior?"
"Three times, my uncle."
"Mention them."
"I threatened my older cousin sister with a knife. I stoned a boy from the neighborhood until his head bled. And I also fought with my cousin who is older than me."
"What did I say about fighting?"

"You said it is wrong as it breeds contempt between friends and spoils the peace in the neighborhood."

"What did you do today?"

"I fought with my cousin who is older than me."

"And?"

"And threatened to go and fetch a table knife and stab him."

"What prevented you from doing all this?"

"Other children stopped me."

"Now?"

"Now I plead for mercy. I won't repeat my bad behavior again."

"What do you expect me to do?"

"To punish me and pardon me."

"I say no! I can't soil my hands by laying them on someone who threatens to stab and kill others. Go away now! And never put your foot here again! Do you hear me?"

I think I will forget about Sibongiseni and the incident, but can't. The blood bond attaches us so severely and can't be broken easily. I can imagine my nephew entering the yard where his mother is renting a room. The room has one bed, one oak chair, one washing basin, one grass broom, and one small table with dishes, a primus stove, and a paraffin lamp. His mother is sitting on the chair and two aunts from the village have come to look for a job in the city and are now sitting on the bed breastfeeding their bawling babies.

The boy throws himself on his mother's bed and cries hysterically, his face buried in the bedspread. "I have been chased off from uncle's home, in Mthatha… my only uncle… whom I love most." I can imagine him repeating these words to his mother.

His mother puts her hands on her breasts and stares in bewilderment.

"You mean him? Doesn't he fear bad luck and the anger of our fathers? Or now he realizes that he is educated and we are not? He has forgotten that my mother and his mother are daughters of one man and one woman......" Indeed a pathetic background. My nephew grew up literally on the streets. His mother held him against her breast as she sold fruit at her stall daily in the streets at Ngangelizwe. As Sibongiseni grew up, he had to battle constantly with flies from a nearby dustbin. Every day, as he grew up, he crawled at the feet of passers-by until he reached the age to begin school.

His mother's belly had already begun to bulge as she left the now-closed TV factory in the small industrial area called Vulindlela Heights because of underpaying and frequent workers' strikes. So, she was still new on the streets when she gave birth to her first and only child, and already she was in her late thirties.

In Ngangelizwe, in an area known as backward because it is situated at the extreme end of the township, always behind in development and popular for its low rents, Sibongiseni sees and hears many things. He sees many muddy and smelly streets of red clay soil which have dams in the rainy seasons, and the corrugated walls of mud and thatched huts.

He watches as shebeen queens punish their "misbehaving" clients with sjamboks, and sees fighters who fight with no one separating them, until the weak run away or their injured bodies hit the dust. He also sees young women who have liberated themselves from their men and who are ever ready to use a pocket knife or their fists to get themselves out of trouble. These women don't need the assistance of magistrate courts to exact child maintenance grants from their lovers. The child hears the unrestrained cries of the fighters as they tear at one another.

I feel sorry for my nephew and for the way he is growing up, and I also feel sorry for my cousin. I want to help my cousin raise the child. When Sibongiseni's mother arrives at my house in Northcrest to ask why I sent Sibongiseni away, I am ready with an explanation. "Although I am obliged to be an uncle to the boy, there are now two other things involved in this that are at risk: the safety of my children, and the peace between my family and our neighbors. My children have only one life, and once that life is taken, it can't be replaced. Sibongiseni's behavior threatens all these things," I say.

Sibongiseni's mother just turns away and says nothing. She turns to the pavement on the street to sell. She now must discipline the boy herself. Sibongiseni's father deserted them long ago.

The blood bond that exists between my cousin and me has lived on healthily until the occurrence of this problem; where she seems to doubt my position. From the days when we were still big children herding my father's livestock on the veld together until now, when we are staying in Mthatha, we didn't hesitate to support each other when there was need.

She wouldn't spare her energy and fighting tactics on the grazing land when she saw me engage in a fight with another boy—which was common especially with the bullies who enjoyed making life difficult for others. She wouldn't hesitate to deliver heavy punches with her fists, bite well with her teeth, or wield the stick with great dexterity. Recognizing this man-graded service of hers to me, I would find myself bound to call her "my brother." I did the same for her in our adult life as we lived in the small city of Mthatha, especially in the 1980s when she worked at a factory that was pestered by workers' strikes which often subjected its employees to police detention and suspension from work with no pay. Thanking my support, she would loudly say, "It is good not to be born alone." With this, she meant that I acted with the love of a blood brother to his own sister—more than the love of a cousin that I was. Which pleased me greatly.

Memories of these events suddenly revive themselves in my mind and touch my heart as I see her leave our place heading for her rented room in the township with a misguided feeling that I am no longer strong in our bond. She has not yet arrived at her place as I park my small second-hand car next to the gate of their yard. I have come to inquire about Sibongiseni's progress at school, which is actually my routine. Sibongiseni has, for the first time, forgotten to bring his test and assignment books during his visit to our place—for me to assess his progress in studies and do commendation or motivation. "Being someone's uncle is like a birthmark: it doesn't change, it doesn't end; no matter what," I say to myself while I park my car, feeling the strength of the bonds of attachment in spite of Sibongiseni's unacceptable behavior and the severity of my anger.

Indeed, beside this particular event, I am still loyal to the blood bond. I still cannot talk of myself without referring to my kinship. The bonds of attachment are still very strong. I am prepared to help Sibongiseni with whatever he needs from me, but away from my home and my children—unless he shows a concrete change in his ways.

Mmap Nonfiction and Academic books

If you have enjoyed *Conundrums and Other Essays* consider these other fine **Mmap Nonfiction and Academic books** from *Mwanaka Media and Publishing:*

Cultural Hybridity and Fixity by Andrew Nyongesa
Tintinnabulation of Literary Theory by Andrew Nyongesa
South Africa and United Nations Peacekeeping Offensive Operations by Antonio Garcia
A Case of Love and Hate by Chenjerai Mhondera
A Cat and Mouse Affair by Bruno Shora
The Scholarship Girl by Abigail George
The Gods Sleep Through It All by Wonder Guchu
PHENOMENOLOGY OF DECOLONIZING THE UNIVERSITY: Essays in the Contemporary Thoughts of Afrikology by Zvikomborero Kapuya
Africanization and Americanization Anthology Volume 1, Searching for Interracial, Interstitial, Intersectional and Interstates Meeting Spaces, Africa Vs North America by Tendai R Mwanaka
Africa, UK and Ireland: Writing Politics and Knowledge Production Vol 1 by Tendai R Mwanaka
Writing Language, Culture and Development, Africa Vs Asia Vol 1 by Tendai R Mwanaka, Wanjohi wa Makokha and Upal Deb
Zimbolicious: An Anthology of Zimbabwean Literature and Arts, Vol 3 by Tendai Mwanaka
Drawing Without Licence by Tendai R Mwanaka

HIV AND AIDS IN ZIMBABWE: A REVIEW ON THE RELATIONSHIP BETWEEN PERCEPTION OF MASCULINITY AMONGST UNMARRIED YOUNG MEN AND THEIR SEXUAL BEHAVIORS by Lucas Kudakwashe Muvhiringi

AFRICA'S CONTEMPORARY FOOD INSECURITY: SELF-INFLICTED WOUNDS THROUGH MODERN VENI VIDI VICI AND LAND GRABBING by Nkwazi Mhango

I Can't Breathe and other Essays by Zvikomborero Kapuya

Ayabacholization Classroom In My Life: The Longest Shortcut To University Education by Peter Ateh-Afec Fossungu

Gathering Evidence by Tendai Rinos Mwanaka

Best New African poets 10th anniversary: Interviews and Reviews by Tendai Rinos Mwanaka

In the footsteps of a Bipolar Life by Ambrose Cato George and Abigail George

No Business Like Love Business by Peter Atec-Afec Fossungu

RE-ENGINEERING UNDER-EXPLORED RENEWABLE ENERGY by Blessing Barnet Chiniko

Manifestations of trauma in the post-2000 Zimbabwean Literature by Nyarai Maria Kanyemba

Donald Trump's Second Coming: Is Democracy, Dead, Dying or Alive by Tendai Rinos Mwanaka

HISTORY IN HISTORY OF AMBAZONIA RESISTENCE by Peter Afec-Ateh Fossungu

Zimbolicious 10th Anniversary Anthology: New and Collected Non-fictions by Tendai Rinos Mwanaka

Letters to Dariah by Rumbi Chen

THE KALEIDOSCOPE OF LIFE: Essays on Identity and Indigenous Knowledge Systems by Sithembe Isaac Xhegwana
Pulse of the Sub-Saharan Dunes by Moussa Traore

Upcoming books

https://facebook.com/MwanakaMediaAndPublishing

www.ingramcontent.com/pod-product-compliance
Lightning Source LLC
Chambersburg PA
CBHW050350030726
47503CB00008B/2713